Dear Dr

Thanks for —ing so much for me. You are a gracious and giving

we of the forsaken world...

Soul. Looking forward to our future collaborations,

we of the forsaken world...

KIRAN BHAT

IGUANA

Publisher: Meghan Behse
Editor: Lee Parpart
Front cover design: Meghan Behse
Map design: Kyle Poirier (thepeartree.ca)

ISBN 978-1-77180-366-3 (paperback)
ISBN 978-1-77180-367-0 (epub)
ISBN 978-1-77180-368-7 (Kindle)

This is an original print edition of *we of the forsaken world...*

Introduction

expect the individual reader to first be consumed by the vignettes of each individual's story, but over the course of the novel to realise that four greater storylines are being told, and to become swept into these greater worlds. The reader is expected to handle this balancing act of individualising the narrators, constructing the stories of each world, and most importantly, being tossed back and forth through four localities the way technology is currently transcending our definitions of place.

You are free to take all of this into consideration as you read my novel or enter into its world without any introduction. Although this book does make a lot of aesthetic demands on the reader, I hope that those demands are justified by its larger aims. I want to throw out our pre-twenty-first century assumptions about how a place can be narrated, and guide readers to think globally. This includes attention to the narratives of those who are so far unable to participate in global culture, societies set in the parts of the world written off as backwards, which happen to also be the nations where innovation and our new humanity will be at its ripest and most capable of flourishing. Although the geographic locations described in this novel are fictitious, readers will notice some similarities to existing regions of the world, from the villages and metropolitan centres of the so-called developing world to those few remote places on Earth where societies have flourished without contact with the rest of humanity until recent years. Without referencing any specific nations or peoples, this novel nevertheless sets up resonances with the populations of many different parts of the world where whole groups of people are living full lives. This fictional world is designed to evoke those lives and pull those people out of obscurity in a way that honours the fullness of their being. By rendering fictional worlds of my imagination, I also wanted to make it clear that I did not want to speak for anyone who wasn't myself. Whether they belong to isolated tribes in the middle of Papua or the highest skyscrapers of Moscow, people have a fundamental right to speak for themselves. I wanted to imagine a world of my own, an alternative version of our globe, that allowed me to tell the stories of people who resemble those who reside on our own topography, without running the risk of pretending a story of theirs happens to be mine.

Maps

THE TRIBE OF THE SILT: A giant river flows through one of the biggest rainforests in the world. Before the government ordered that large expanses of the rainforest be cut down for the sake of industrialisation of the nearby provinces, the land was known to be one of the most biodiverse of the world. Various types of monkeys, sloths, parrots, frogs, fish, river dolphins, turtles, and insects live in the forests, rivers, and mangroves. As of late, media attention has focused on the disappearance of the bodies of several workers who are said to have been taken from the site where magnolia is being logged. Far beyond the reach of current public information, there exists beyond this site another enclave, where a tribe not yet discovered by the rest of humanity lives. They are said to be ancestor-worshippers who live together on one side of the river, in big huts held up by logs under twigged roofs. They sleep, often one man with several wives and their children, over the bones of their deceased. The chief of the tribe is said to have the biggest hut of them all. Due to conquests and wars between the tribes, the Tribe of the Silt has become an amalgamation of all the tribes that once populated the entire rainforest. There are about fifty or so members of the tribe left, and they live deep within the dense canopies of the forest, so far untouched by industry. It is for this reason that, in the eyes of the outside world, people consider the rainforest to be entirely extinct of its indigenous people.

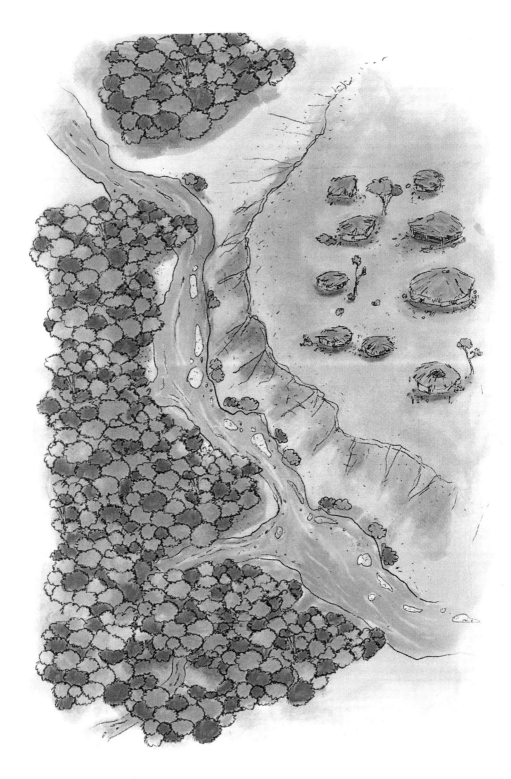

A GLOBAL VILLAGE: There is a bend in the grasslands where only one road leads to the rest of the world. Large expanses of the land are empty, but once one crosses a small creek and travels further through the dust, one can see the occasional man or woman walking on what they call the main road. All along this road, small shops have grown like polyps. In the morning, the inhabitants of the village stay at home, eat breakfast, and exchange gossip. During the day, they commute barefoot or in sandals to the road, to sell each other a wide range of goods, from mobiles and cabbages to sugar cane and various snacks. Cell phone technology has reached this community in relatively recent years, and the community is suffering growing pains as a result of this change. Many people spend their days inside their stores, hemmed in by their goods, playing random games on their phones. Each community has about twenty houses. Only one of the dwellings was built recently: an apartment complex made by the government, with grey brick walls that have yet to be painted. Others live in the mud huts that pimple the grasslands. These are mostly one-storey dwellings, each with two rooms and a thatched roof. Regardless of their small size, each house usually consists of a room with a television and a cot and another room with a cot for sleeping, and an outside expanse with a toilet and cooking area. Housewives band together to cook various meals and look after the children, while the children spend their time playing games with each other or alone on their phones. The most famous (or infamous) man of the village was once the richest, known for having the biggest cow estate in the greater area. He is no longer in this world, but his daughter tends to his cows and delivers their milk to the entire community to this day.

THE LAKE OF THE SACRED SALT: There was once a small city known as one of the great cultural centres of its country. This small city was famed for its lake, which held special healing powers. One dip in its waters was said to cure almost any illness. The area housed many important writers and artists, and was frequented by tourists for its chocolate, beer, and distinctive style of blown glass. As of late, the lake has dominated world headlines due to an industrial spill that killed 2,386 people. The catastrophe occurred when a water cooler at a poorly managed pesticide plant malfunctioned, funneling a cloud of cumin-coloured gas into a residential area of this important industrial hub in the middle of the night. For weeks, entire streets were shrouded with plastic bags covering the bodies of the dead, and the trees were stained yellow for years. The damage extended from the suburbs to downtown, affecting stores, bars, fruit markets, and the small brick houses behind and between them. Five weeks after this environmental catastrophe, the CEO of the pesticide company, who had always claimed that the industrial spill was out of their hands, diminished the event by referring to it as "just an incident." That phrase spiraled around the fire at a vigil, until it became the name of the tragedy, the Incident. News reporters and journalists from inside the country and abroad poured into the lakeside community in the interest of highlighting a tragedy very few had learned about.

BLACK CITY: There is a capital like any other of the rising world. From an aerial view, one sees apartment complexes and skyscrapers in all directions. It is only when one zooms in closer that one sees slums between the buildings, tin hovels with the occasional blanket or bed sheet for a wall. There are parts of the city where the slums cover the ground like the giant folds of an umbrella punctured at its side. In those holes are usually houses from a different era, painted red or yellow, baby blue, or eggshell green. Black City boasts the Great Founder's Plaza, which is famous for having the first statue of the country's first president. Most people visit this area to take a picture of the biggest cathedral in the region and the colonial buildings around it. Some also visit the market in the city's north end to buy cheap electronics and clothes. The people of the city journey to its modern side to shop in the commercial malls, work in the skyscrapers, and eat in fast food chains that are generally avoided by the tourists who visit the historic area. Very rarely do people visit the slums or the attractions inside of it. There is a superstition that every homeless person of the city believes: if one crosses to the other side of the statue of the Great Founder and does not cover the path behind them with a thin line of salt, their soul will be ripe for the taking from a one-armed shadow who works for the Devil himself.

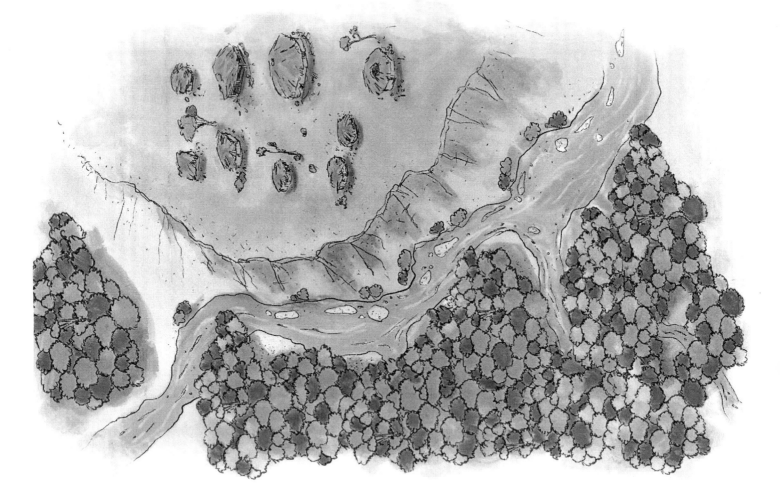

we of the forsaken world...

Translations

A cloud of yellow gas from the pesticide plant had descended over the ring of houses around the lake and killed thousands of our people. My only son, his wife, and their daughter were sent to the hospital. A few days later, I received news from a nurse that they were dead. Shrouded corpses were piled along the streets. Friends had thrown out their dogs with the soil. The smell in town was of flesh and mould and pee. The journalist asked if my wife was religious. I had nothing to say.

The journalist stopped looking up and down my face. He scribbled notes on the bottom of his page with an unlit cigarette in his mouth. He had chosen to conduct these interviews at one of the cafés by the lake. In the eighties, the golden facades of the lakeside buildings were the colour of caramel, and the homemade chocolate sold on the waterfront tasted better than rum. These days, the plastic outlines cleared of the bodies made the sidewalks look like the inside of a furniture store, and flies swarmed between the brick walls and the racks full of postcards. On the other side of the boardwalk area was the neighbourhood of run-down apartments my son and his family had chosen to move into. I had no reservations when they decided to move there. Our cottage was dilapidating, and I knew my son was often bored living in our tree-lined suburb. The apartment they found was barely the size of our second floor, but it was cheap, central, and close to their work. They said they would visit once a week. A weekly visit was more than enough.

This side of the boardwalk at least was cleaned up. In my son's new neighbourhood, the military was still checking for bodies in apartment buildings. These were not the soldiers from my days in the army. They were wearing the inflated garments of astronauts. They stared at the living as if they had come back from space. I had spent a lot of my last few days by the boardwalk. This was why I knew all this.

This journalist did not look like the kind of man who would work for the paper, *Our Nation*. They were usually northerners of the tall and pale sort. He was a man of medium height. He had the features of someone from here, but his eyes were green, and he spoke none of our language. His hair was greying. His blazer, pants, socks, and shoes were all black. He always kept his back straight. I found this a very northerner thing to do. He repeated his question, slowly, like he was speaking to a child.

"What … happened … to your … wife … during … the … Incident?"

"Nothing … nothing much," I responded. "Tragedy comes … people change. She become religion. I become smoking."

"I didn't … understand," the journalist said. I switched to my language.

"We all change when tragedy strikes. My sweet dear darling used to pray once a week, now she goes to the church at six in the morning, even while the doors are closed. I go through a carton of cigarettes in a day. An entire carton, in one day. I used to only smoke when my brother visited town."

The journalist patted the dandruff out of his hair.

"You answered in … again," he said. "I think I … some words, but I won't be able to … this if you don't…"

I did not know how to speak our national language. I used to listen well, but I did not have the energy to struggle. I even lacked the force to sigh. I lifted my cigarette pack from the table and showed it to him.

"Do …. you … need … a lighter?" he asked. My wife told me once she never knew if I was staring at her these days or at something behind her. I must have given him one of these stares. He found his own lighter and pack of cigarettes in his briefcase.

We paused to smoke. The black circles of his tape recorder rolled on. The fifty-year-old posters on the wall watched us. The server was cleaning the coffee table and switching TV channels. The coffee machine made the most noise out of us all. Our table was by a window facing the road. A few people passed the window. They were loud, built men, their arms stained with petrol. They must have come from stores on the parallel streets where tires were sold and cars were repaired. Behind them came some women, heads covered with polka-dot or striped scarves, or with dark black ones. They all stared openly at the journalist. Tourists hadn't come since the Incident.

"My mother … she … told me … of this place … when I was a … child…"

He went on using words bigger than any I knew. I would have loved to tell him there were many things to see in our city. It was famed for its precious blown glass. The most famous store of its kind was four storeys, at the centre of the intersection between the ring road and the main avenues leading up a hill. If people were not looking for souvenirs, they could eat our style of chocolate, or go to the saunas towards the north, as the lake was famed over centuries for healing problems of the back. The university on the other side of the lake was one of the best in the nation. Our textiles and products went all over the country, all over the world. We were so much more than our calamity. We were a vibrant town mentioned in many great novels, with a history of hundreds of years.

These were all the things I could never express in the language he knew. He realised I understood little. His eyes skipped to the end of his thoughts. Silence came again, and I made a trip to the bathroom. The window next to the sink peered towards the lake. The sun kissed the cloud hats upon the green hills goodbye. It left warm flickers of orange around the water's edge. It would have been pretty to reflect on, if the lake had not been powdered yellow and dotted with the bodies of dead fish.

"There are few parts of our country as beautiful as the north side of this lake," I reminded him when I returned. It was a good place to fish or to picnic with the family, if he had one. He sighed around his cigarette. I changed languages and repeated slowly, "North ... lake ... nice..."

He smothered his cigarette against the black table.

"I really should have hired ..." he said. "But, the advertisements did say that the interviews were to be ... for a national ..."

Yes, yes. *Our Nation.* A newspaper which rarely represented the needs of people from the south, and yet the only one willing to hear our voices at all. I gave him the stare my wife complained about.

"It would have been nice ... very good ... if my mother had ... the time to teach me your language. She comes ... from here..."

I could see that from his skin tone and curly hair.

"But my father is from the north…"

I could tell that as well, from his round cheeks, and wide green eyes.

"I was raised far from here … far … far … and moved to the capital for work … work … I've never been to this city before … or any city around here, for that…"

He should have known our language, regardless. Did no one have pride in their culture? My son didn't teach his daughter a single word. He said it wasn't understood in the city where he worked. I thought it was luck when he was transferred back home. When I was in the army, this region had no signs in other languages, and its children were taught in our script and knew only their tongue. Often my granddaughter didn't understand a single thing I said. I had taught her the words for "water," "pine," "pumpkin," and "comb." I should have taught her much more.

The journalist saw I was thinking of them. His eyes lost their drunkenness of thought. He straightened his back and offered me his pen. His eyes were sad and his words jumbled and he was hard to understand. It was when he asked his question that he spoke like someone on the radio.

"How … how does it feel … feel … to know your family is … gone … dead … over?"

"I don't know," I said.

"Do you miss your granddaughter?"

"Yes," I said. The words to be said in my language were, 'Of course.' I remembered the morning of their last weekend visit when she woke me at the foot of the bed. I told her I wanted to sleep. She exclaimed, *Look!* She flittered her feet on the hardwood floor and jumped in the air and showed off the calluses on her toes. I told her she was going to be the best dancer I knew. Then I sent her back to bed, for the sake of any family member not yet awake. I was planning to buy her a new pair of dance shoes for her next sleepover. The next day, she appeared to be more interested in the anatomy of caterpillars, and dragged me into the garden for me to see them.

I remembered when my wife and I searched for her body in the pile of corpses. Hers was the face being eaten by the maggots. For many days after, no words came out of my mouth.

"And your daughter-in-law?"

"Yes, yes," I said. My daughter-in-law often hunched her back and held her knees when she sat. It looked like she was preparing to warm an egg. I always wanted to joke with her about it. Afraid I would offend her, I never did. My eyelids were flinching because I was wondering why I never grew courage over things so minute.

"And your son? Don't you miss him?"

The words I wanted to say were, 'How could I not?' I didn't get to see him. The hospital had cremated all of its corpses when I visited. They did such things without the relatives' permission, too. What an excuse, that there had been too many bodies. I spent the entire evening wondering if he had even died in a bed. I thought of the last words we had exchanged. Much like me, he was a collector of coins. I had been recently gifted a coin that was minted around the time of my military days by an old friend who had found it in a closet. I made a promise to my boy to give the coin to him the following weekend. It became a date that would never pass.

I had not said anything, and the journalist sighed, one too many times. I banged the table and stood.

"You are nothing but a rude northerner coming to a land where you speak nothing and expect us to accommodate to you."

I threw his notebook at the poster nearby and knocked over one of the cups.

"Do you know how many nights I prepared for this interview, and now, I cannot say anything?"

The server reacted as quickly as a disturbed cat and rushed to the table. She was too afraid to speak.

"My son is dead. His family is dead. None of them are coming back. My wife and I will die knowing that our family will not continue. And who is to blame? Who is to blame? The most corrupt government in the world chose to build a pesticide plant here, knowing that it would be cheaper. This is a government that has done nothing but damn our region since the day it was annexed. Even to this day, the head of that company refuses to call our tragedy anything more than an 'incident.' Do you know how that feels? Do you? Do you?"

The journalist stood as well. He took the napkins under his beer and used them to pick up the broken glass. I wanted to kick him as he crawled.

"Do you know how any of this feels?" I squatted down and yelled. "Do you? Do you?"

The journalist sat up and slapped a palm against his ear.

"He cannot understand a word you are saying," said the server. I knew. Whether it was in our language or not, he could not understand. The server brought a trash can. I handed her a bill for the damages. I went to another table and smoked. I also ordered a beer for the sake of the server. The journalist had blinked little and shown no emotion during my entire speech. I could have asked him if he had colleagues who interviewed in our language. I did not.

(The Grandfather)

I took out my wallet.
I reached for the coin meant for my son,
and held it under my palm.

(The Immigrant)

This guy who *pissed me off*, he may not have known it, but if my brother was still in the city, he would have had to hop out of here with both of his legs broke. I was imagining the cracking sounds long after the *second* beer, and the *third* one, and after more people had come. This bar was always packed with international students, but they weren't made to sit at the stools, and they didn't have to stand in line to be seated; they *just got in.* Maybe if I had the money to buy high-end brands and not market-priced knockoffs, maybe if I lived in New Town or by Galaxy Mall, I wouldn't have to go to the only place near our shop that had a happy hour. My paycheque in a day was good enough for three beers at most, but people were flicking their cigarette ashes all over my clothes, like they thought my shirt was *so cheap* I could buy another one if it got soiled. I ordered another beer. I hadn't eaten all day, and no one wants to take care of a drunk either, so I ordered some fries. It was ten at night, and if brother was not home, I had no reason to return early. They were turning on something louder and electro, a pop song brother put on when we got drunk together. I got to see all of these girls shaking their thighs, wearing miniskirts, tossing around their long hair. I kept looking at them, and they kept looking away, *like always.* One of those girls had a cross around her neck, and it was making me think too much about mother, and not in a good way, *not in a good way at all.* I bought another beer.

"Is that guy just going to sit there and order the cheap beers all night?"

"Shh ... be nice."

I didn't see who said it, but I heard it, and proving them wrong was worth more than what I earned for a few hours manning brother's shop. I ordered one of the most expensive craft beers on the menu. I usually like beers that are bitter on the tongue, but they didn't have that many local crafts in the first place, and the domestic ones, like the one with the picture of the crown on it, tasted a bit too much like water with a little hops touched in.

"Did you hear the way he said craft? Kuh-raw-fuht! Who says it like that?"

"Shh ... he's going to hear you."

"I doubt he's understanding a thing."

I was understanding that I needed some gin. Like, *really* needed some gin.

The good thing about these bars is that you will end up meeting a stranger who knows nothing about you and so you can shout what's on your mind. I didn't like the way the guy sitting next to me was tapping his loafers, *completely* off beat from the way the song was being played, but with what I was dealing with, with what I was *always* dealing with, I couldn't believe how happy it made me feel that there was someone who would smile at me when we stared at each other for so long.

"Finally!"

"What?"

"The jerk's gone!"

"I'm sorry, I'm not following."

He pointed to his ear like it was too loud. I pulled him by the shirt and he almost fell into my lap.

"I said the guy was a jerk. Going on and on about beers… What's a beer to anyone? We have mouths, and we drink. Who says things like that to someone's face, someone's face they don't even know?"

This new guy was sitting up and nodding a lot but with his eyes wide and his teeth showing.

"Do you understand what I mean? You have to know what I mean."

The guy shook his head and shrugged.

"I'm sorry, I'm not following you. Where do you come from?"

What would my brother have done? He would have had a laugh about it, talked up our town, made a friend. Well, my brother was home for the first time in years, and I was at this bar, without him, and so I did not act as my brother would have. I swivelled my chair around and talked to someone else. I forget what we talked about — was it about his job or mine? — and I forget what he looked like — was he a younger guy with a beer belly or the one wearing sunglasses on his forehead? — but he did pour beer all over my shoes, my worthless, torn-up tennis shoes with stuffing coming out of the sides, and when I took them off and threw them away, I was ordered to keep them on. And then I tried to dance, but I wasn't dancing well, because the clashing colours were everywhere, red and green and blue and red again, and the music pounded so much into the brain that it wasn't possible to process anything at all. The girls were all drunk. The local girls were shaking their shoulders to the bass-heavy music, but there were also foreigners — girls who wore little black dresses and who bent all the way down to the ground when they danced, covering the skin of their hips with their purses. They looked like the girls in music videos, the way they arched their legs and shook every part of their body, flirting with the waiters like they should have been flirting with me. The ones I approached walked away, and one girl *had the nerve* to shake her palm in front of her nose. The random person I talked to had gone to the toilet, or left, and it was never any fun being alone at a bar. The waiter asked me something while I was leaving. I made some excuse about going on a cigarette break, and the next thing I knew I was on the street.

Oh, brother, my brother, where would you have gone if you were like me? Certainly he would have gone home, not home as in the home where mother and father and sister live, where he already was, but he would have long boarded one of the buses going to Orange Town from the Great Founder's Plaza. Between here and the plaza were a lot of big avenues, and in between those big avenues were small alleys, and the only way to get there was to take one of those streets leading away from the skyscrapers and hope you were going the right way. I walked down an alley where a lot of guys handed out flyers for their clubs. I couldn't tell if they were offering cheap beer, girls, or drugs, but you had to pay an entrance fee to get in. The alley behind it had a bunch of liquor and cigarette and junk-food stores. I turned left when I realised it was curving towards those steps, and on those steps was a guy getting a blow job, but the alley I took wasn't lit so I had to use walls to feel where I was walking. Somehow, I got to a main avenue, where there were so many lights I was squinting, and I almost tripped over a homeless kid. Straight down that avenue was the plaza, where I could see the statue of the Great Founder. The plaza was bustling with aggression. A guy working at a restaurant threw menus at people's faces, a vendor who carried shoes in a plastic bag shoved them at me, cars honked, and random people pushed and rushed and shoved.

Without brother at home, what was the point of it all? I never liked loud noises, I never liked so many people, and I swore I was going to throw up, right in the face of a girl who was exiting the bakery wearing sunglasses. Father said I was the strongest man in the family; mother said I was the man in the family who knew how to care for someone. Both were convinced that brother needed me, and everyone was convinced that the family needed more money and that I was old enough to work. I should have told them that I loved sitting on their couch with my head on mother's lap playing on my phone, and I missed being fattened up by mother's cooking, the cassavas simmering in the shrimp sauce, chicken fried so the oil wetted your bones. I had father's shop to work at, the gym nearby if I wanted to build muscle, and my sisters lived far away, but I didn't mind listening to them when they took their weekend trips from their homes to come see us. Why didn't I tell mother and father I never wanted to go abroad? I threw up, not in front of the girl, *thank God,* but in one of the trash cans in an alley behind one of the two-storey chain restaurants. Some of the people getting out of a midnight matinee stared at me, and I flipped them off.

I felt a lot better after throwing up, good enough to walk all the way to where I could see the statue of the Great Founder salute the street, the city hall building behind it. It wasn't a pretty plaza, because of all the plastic bags and used napkins around it and the homeless people who sat around the statue or near the market on its northern side, but there was something about it that came alive at night, like the lamps around the old stucco buildings where the buses came and went, transporting people to and from the suburbs and the centre. The buildings had an almost fleshy appearance, like the colour of mother's socks. I was usually working when the lights came on, but brother said it was a good place to be during the evening; the tourists were too afraid of what their guidebooks called unsafe, and the place was filled with students waiting for the buses to take them home. I didn't know why he kept telling me to talk to students when I never went to school and liked it best when we went to the bars and clubs together. I walked a little south to see that all the buses going to Orange Town were gone. I checked the signs again, and tried to talk to some of the drivers. The only one who responded told me to check the time. I didn't have a watch, and my phone was long dead, but even if I was completely sober I would have cursed him and his balding crown and his cunt of a mother. I don't remember if we fought or not, but I do remember having a sharp pain in the jaw.

What would brother have done if he had missed the bus, not made it home, was a little drunk? Well, brother went to our real home, didn't consider buying a plane ticket for me, all because he needed someone to man the shop. To think I loved my brother so much, gave him my spare money, introduced him to girls, and *he left me like this?* At least if I was going to spend a night out, I was going to spend it with a girl. There were plenty of them standing around the statue wearing fishnet stockings and high heels. I asked one of them to take me home. She had her hair permed and was sitting on the statue steps with her legs spread apart for everyone to see. No joke. When I spoke to her, she stood up and pretended to wait for a bus. I put my hand over the stain on my shirt and shouted some things to the other girls. The ones who weren't paying attention hurried away, but a girl I chased stopped walking away, turned back to look at me with her hand cupped around her ear, and claimed she didn't get the language of hicks.

How I ended up on the other side of an alley, one between the plaza and the avenue I crossed before, with my hand against a brick wall, pulling up some girl by her already ripped blouse, I wasn't sure. When she had seen me, she scooted as close as possible to the wall, hiding herself under one of those blankets they give out on luxury buses. She shouldn't have done that, because that was the move all the other girls made in the history of my life, and I wasn't going to let *her* get away with it. I wasn't going to touch her in *that* way, but I liked that when I tore her blanket off, she curled into herself like one of those animals that liked to play dead, and when I breathed in her face, she snivelled, and when I pulled her up, she was struggling to free herself from under my weight. She didn't like the smell on my breath more than anyone else did, I guessed. I stared at her and decided to ask her some things.

"Do you think I'm fat? Do you think I'm ugly? Do you think I look like some kind of tapir?"

The funny thing was that I wanted her to say I looked like a tapir, because they were common in our country, much more than they were here, and when I was younger I was chubby and round-faced with a long nose, and even up to the day I left for the city, a lot of my friends called me Calf. *Hey, Calf, can you pass me that water? Hey, Calf, when are you giving me that money back?* No one here knew me as Calf. She looked up at me with fear in her eyes.

"I don't know what a tapir is," she said. I saw someone passing between the alleys and I pulled myself a bit closer to her. She looked down and away from me when she spoke again. "You're actually handsome."

I slapped her because I didn't want to be lied to and I didn't want to be handsome, at least not tonight.

"Don't lie to me," I said. "You better tell me the truth, or I'll do something much worse than slap you."

"I can't understand," she said, and she closed her eyes like she wanted this strange encounter to be over with, and I was *this close* to putting her down, this close to at least screaming, *just call me a Tapir Calf, I want to be a calf,* but somewhere in the middle of this all I felt someone staring at me, and before I could react, I got a hard kick between my legs. She ran, screaming something about a shadow, that the shadow had come, that the Devil's shadow was here, and I wanted to run myself, but I was in a lot of pain, and then a foot was pressing into my balls while I was kneeling over. My eyes couldn't adjust to whatever light there was in the darkness, but I could see that there was someone in front of me, someone with the breasts and clipped curves of a starving woman, a broad nose, and hungry cheekbones. A fluffy jacket covered her body, and her eyes stared out of the pelt like a wolf's. If the Devil had a shadow, it would have looked something like this. She was going to kill me, I thought, or take some sharp knife and cut me up, but she lifted her foot from my groin and pulled me up like I had the other woman.

"Do you know what happens to men who violate women?" she asked. I told her I was just fucking around, and she took her right arm and flung me against a part of the wall where a sewer pipe was leaking. "Absolutely nothing, actually. Most women know what it's like to be touched in all the wrong places, but most say nothing. Do you know why that is?"

"Do you know how happy I would be if a woman touched me in those kinds of places?"

She kicked me again. I stared up the sleeve on the left side of her jacket and saw there was nothing there.

"You are a pathetic man," she said, and she spat towards me. A siren blared in the distance. For a moment I thought she might be scared off by the noise, but she kept her foot close to my groin. "No, do not speak. How I wish I had the energy inside of myself to deal with you, but Death has been chasing men of much darker hearts for a much longer time than it has been chasing you. Yes, Death has quite a long and distinguished list, and for a man who doesn't even have the courage to be honest with himself without drink in his veins, you fall quite low on it."

I couldn't stand, and she laughed.

"Weak in the mind, weak in the spirit, weak in the legs. I feel sorry for those who raised you."

I didn't. The people in my life were *good people*. They were considered poor in our country, and could be seen as lower-middle-class or poorer-than-poor in a city like this, depending on which neighborhood you happened to be living in, and they had sacrificed everything for me to make sure I had just enough of an education to be able to work a decent job, or just enough money so that it would be more than a dream to move out. I wasn't proving them right this night, but I stared at the graffiti on the other side of the wall that I hadn't noticed before, the words "We shall resist" written in a bold black. I pushed myself up using the pipe and leaned my back against the wall so I could stand up, but I was so dizzy I was seeing her jacket and the words and the concrete in blur. I was going to fall down again, but it was important I at least said a few things.

"You know nothing about my family..."

The pain in my groin had gone away for a bit, only to return when I was standing.

"My family is good people ... My family is great people ... I miss my family ... I miss my home so much..."

I was sitting down, collapsing in my own words, about to cry, because I had said *just a little too much,* and I was saying things that made me hate myself *just that much.* She was crouching over me, making it hard to avoid her smell, like branches burning in spit.

"Your eyes are fluttering back and forth like the wings of a hummingbird," she said. "I once saw a devil, now I see an angel. Your eyes are creative, intelligent, caring and warm. Why are you doing such nonsense in the middle of a gutter where not even the sun chooses to shine?"

She also asked some questions which sober me wouldn't have understood, *let alone the dead drunk one.*

"Are you working for Looker? How much did he pay you? What did he ask of you? No, you wouldn't. He picks people of your level of hopelessness to do his bidding, but it isn't like his men are the only ones who go out of their way to make the souls of women into shade."

I was starting to see it, this Post-it note that was taped onto her jacket that she was taking off and reading, because I was looking at it, not because she needed to read it.

"I am back in town tomorrow, my dirty little handshake. Come meet me at the Regency by Galaxy Mall at seven. I'll be sitting at the lobby. We'll go in my room, and you'll take off that sheet. I got some clothes for you that you would like. Just in case, a few of my boys will be there to help make sure they fit ... Looking on, Looker."

I was reaching for the note because I thought she was tired of reading and wanted me to take over, but she crumpled it up and threw it into the gutter. She was standing over the sewer and taking something out of her jacket, but I didn't think it was a gun until I heard the bullets ricochet off the drain and I saw a flashing light illuminating the ground underneath her feet, and I cowered back into the corner with the stained blanket, pushing myself underneath it.

"At least he gave me a day in advance," she said, and she motioned what was in her hand back into her jacket. She sounded like she was smirking, but I could see enough of her face in the headlights of the passing trucks and cars to know that her expression was almost completely blank. It wasn't because I was hammered that she was fading right in front of my eyes; she really was moving in the way that the shadows blurred into the concrete.

"Wait!" I said. "Wait! You said nice things about me. No one says nice things about me. I am caring, I am sensitive, I am a good guy, I am the son my mother wanted me to be. Take me with you. I will help you find this friend of yours. I will help you shoot up more gutters or try on his things. I am good at following orders, ask my brother, and if that's not what you want, I can change. I want to change..."

She was stopping, or she was walking along, or she was standing, or she was running, or she was doing them all at once, at least in front of my two eyes. Suddenly there was a bill in my hands, and it wasn't something I was imagining; she really had handed me some money.

"Take this and go wherever you want, on the condition that I never see you back in this gully again."

"Yes ma'am," I said, and I kissed the bill, then stuffed it in the deepest part of my back pocket, under my cell phone and door keys. I kept my promise to her. I kept my promise to myself. I didn't let anyone touch the bill except for the cab driver on the other side of the movie theatre, and I told the driver to take me to the other side of Orange Town. He didn't want to go at first; he said it would be too unsafe at this time, but I told him I had gone all over town looking for a cab, and I was hungry and I needed to pee, and there was a homeless woman with one arm who was going to fill him up with bullets if he didn't do what I said. Finally, he agreed to take me. I got in and closed my eyes. As the cab moved through the south suburbs, with the skyscraper lights flickering in the distance, I thought about how I was going to do right, how I was going to do something good, and that I didn't care that he was going to hear it, I was going to say it out loud, the way a good lullaby gets stuck in your ear, and your memory never lets it go.

(The Immigrant)

"My mother is good people...

Like the river mist of an early sunrise,
Like the shove of the sand against my feet.

My father is great people...

All the shells I was meant to be gifted,
All the turtle skin meant for me to eat,
with him alone.

I miss them both...

He, the great chief of this tribe,
And the first of his wives, I.

For their sake,
I'm going to become good people too…"

This was meant to be our tale, but ever since our daughter became his sixth wife, he had forgotten me, or pretended to have forgotten me, and not just for many moons, but for almost an entire lifetime. It was going to become worse. I had been outside the wives' tent, gutting the big-mouthed fish for the meal ahead, when the shaman threw black silt powder in a circle outside of the chief's tent, covered the branches of the thatched roof with red berry paste, and shouted that the chief's wife had gone into labour. *Note that she couldn't have been talking about me* … A fire was lit on the other side of the chief's tent. The sun blazed through the finger trees until it began to fade, and men and women came out of their tents to warble their tongues to the spirit, play on catskin drums, and dance to the stacks of smoke curling their black fingers into the sky. We wives made our own little fire inside the tent and sacrificed the guts of several fish, in the hopes that he would have another daughter, and not the son he so wished for.

In the faint light of the fire, the chief's slave did her part to coax the new child into the world. She was one of the chief's humbler daughters, a woman who had lost use of her legs to the demons long before she was of age, and although she couldn't dance, she sat in the darkness and flailed at the air with an umbilical cord preserved for this purpose from another birth. She held the fleshy rope high for all to see. The men beat their fists against their chests, while the women cawed to the spirit of the loins and held their palms to the slave's neck. Then the cry went up. *He has finally had his second son, and not his twelfth girl* ... I held my palms to my eyes, saw the night inside them, then opened my eyes and looked at the moon, which would become the sun the moment the monkeys hooted between the finger trees. I was not close enough to any of these wives to explain why I was leaving the tent, and I noticed that the other four women, without much talk, were themselves leaving in unnamed directions, a secrecy that the foliage of the jungle granted us.

My journey was not long. During my childhood, the river was under a cliff of silt by our tents. During my life it had risen, and it was now separated from our tents by a mere beach of silt. I hid myself under the mangroves to let the water splash against my legs.

There was another who sat on the silt not so far from me. He was the son of my husband and his third wife — more living proof that the chief had long not belonged to me. The boy was hooting not to the spirits but to the monkeys. He was as tall as some of the baboons, and to many of us, about as capable. All anyone had to do was to look at the strange cut over his penis, and the results of his circumcision ceremony would shine over each and every one of our necks. There were other reasons why he always appeared sad, and why he mumbled out loud, whether in the company of the little boys or in line with the warriors. He patted his chest, then the space between us. I scooted over, creating a smear in the silt that looked like a giant crab with two handprints instead of pincers. Whatever he said was lost to my ears. I was not in the mood to interpret his thoughts. *Thank the spirits that I was not going to have to call him chief any time in the near future* ... I sat up with my legs crossed like the arms of a mantis and my arms around them, not wanting to get my body wet in the rising tide. I felt the warm ebb of the river tickling the calluses between my toes.

A hand was reaching through my hair. I was about to slap it out, but the boy had found ants in it with pincers sharper than my nails.

"You should be careful of these insects at your age, mother. You do not want to get sick."

Mother ... I felt flattered that he had addressed me with honour. I glanced briefly at him to notice he was rubbing his face. This boy, shorter than any other young man of his age, with eyes that wandered farther than legs ever could, must have walked along the plants and rocks to avoid being seen, for his feet and legs were laced with small cuts. *The pain of losing one's destiny often manifests physically...*

"I'm such an idiot," he said. He stared at the moon and smacked the sides of his head with his fists. "Idiot, idiot, idiot! I never took it seriously. I thought my father would keep birthing girls. I'm so stupid, stupid, stupid."

To be fair, he had lost his right to the chiefhood the moment he presented himself like a girl at his circumcision ceremony. The mother in me wanted to rub his back, or at the very least alert him to the red dart frog that was hopping precariously close. He began walking up and down the bank, uprooting several of the younger and more tender mangroves from the silt and throwing rocks into the river in front of me.

"I'm not going to be chief," he continued. "All my plans might as well be buried in the silt. At least then the star fruits and papayas would grow well."

My feet had made strong prints in the slick, glossy mud. I kicked them out and sat up straight. I remembered how in my childhood the water reflected the clear colour of a dark day's sky. These days, the water was a strange earthy colour, and its waves pulsated a vomit-like orange hue in the moonlight. Without realising it, I had begun planning a speech to the boy. I would comment on the mangroves to our left and right, how strong their roots remained, no matter how much the river around them had changed. I would command him to look at the talons of the trees on the other side of the river. If they were torn down, would the monkeys no longer climb? Would the sloths no longer sleep at the hilt of the bark? *The world around us is constantly changing, but the purpose of life does not waver...*

He picked up another rock and threw it at the river. The rock jumped thrice. I had the sense he wanted to throw the next rock at me. My words came in another form.

"You know nothing about what it means to be a man, do you?"

He cracked his knuckles before throwing another rock. He reached down to pick up another. The wrinkle of skin left on the head of his penis bulged down as he bent.

Few remembered that he was circumcised at half the traditional age. I supposed my husband had lost too many great warriors in his military campaign eastwards, and while he believed little in the prophecy that his son was destined to be the leader to make the moon kiss the day rather than night, he wanted to take advantage of his son's potential. What he failed to grasp was that the boy was too young to stand the procedure, and the chief's son, in shock or pain or surprise, had *cried*. My husband did his best to cover up the scandal, but rumours spread about how this chief was no leader like his father, and how his son was worse yet. Had it not been for the wealth and land attained by that predecessor, the tribe would have fallen apart.

Neither my husband nor his son was spared humiliation. My husband's error was to never forgive him for simply being a boy. The boy's error was to live his life as if his penis had never been cut.

"I will give you this one clue. If you want others to see you as a man, you must learn to act like one first. A boy who complains and throws temper tantrums is no leader."

The boy did not speak, and we had no time to speak further, since we were interrupted by another of the chief's slaves. This was a man who always stayed by his master's side, a man much older than me, a son of the tree-dwellers who was made a slave after the conquest. His mannerisms spoke of a different culture on the other side of the river. He never used the wild flapping of arms or facial expressions the rest of us used to communicate. He was twice as tall as our chief, had the long, flowing hair we associated with females, and his spear spoke more often than he. He had been named over the course of many battles the Silencer. He had come to the mangroves to pull aside the boy.

"The shaman is having a vision. She has said your name."

They hurried towards the tents. I was alone, the way I had wanted to be before the chief's son and I had met. I thought I would sleep here, away from the other wives, to be comforted by the sadness of solitude rather than the starker pain of no longer having a destiny. Whether I slept or not was not clear to me, but I dreamed in the back of the eyes of once more being in labour, of the chief's slave under me, and as she pulled out a dark-haired, narrow-eyed cub, I felt the chief rub his nose against my forehead, and I heard him congratulate me on our son.

It was I who was then pulled up by my shoulders by the Silencer.

"The chief has called for you."

"What?" I asked. I rubbed my eyes and let the skin of my feet sink further in the sand, to confirm that I was not still dreaming.

"Mhm, come." The Silencer had grabbed my hand and was forcing me through the jungle towards my husband's tent.

"You can let me go. I have walked many times in the jungle, both in the dark and alone."

The Silencer may have had muscles greater than my husband's, but his heart was softer.

"Mhm," he said, and he let me go. We crossed the path in the silt cleared of the finger trees. Each of the tents was the size of its own mound, made up of the branches and trunks of the finger trees. We did not want to wake others, but as our feet rustled the leaves on the ground, several men blinked their eyes open, sprang up and reached for their spears, until they saw it was neither a monkey nor a thief, but the eldest wife of the chief being escorted by his most prized warrior. They kneeled and kissed the earth, something they did rarely when I walked alone.

"How is the shaman?" I asked. He did not have to point far. In a cushion of catskin rugs outside of the fireplace of her tent was the shaman herself. She was a hard woman to look at, caked in callouses and blood, wearing the bones of our ancestors around her neck. Most of her hair had fallen out from all the times she had allowed the spirits to possess her. Her eyes often appeared lifeless, but now, as she thrashed and flailed to herself, they rolled into the back of her head.

"The end, the end!" she suddenly barked in a voice sharp enough to cut vines. "The red tree's feet will fall to new men.

The spirits will attack from inside out. Arrows will strike our kin. They are coming, they are coming! They will kill our chief. They will eat our flesh. The water will wash our bones clean. The land will belong to them. The end, the end! It is coming, our end!"

Somehow, no one else was roused from sleep.

"What is she saying?" I asked. Another man would have given me a more detailed answer, but the Silencer pointed back to the river.

"Mhm."

"Whatever she is saying, it is not good. I am surprised no one else is concerned. Rather, perhaps too many are concerned, and that is why no one is speaking."

Whether he had nothing to say or no desire to open up to me, we had reached the chief's tent, at the center of the path, dwarfed by the canopy of trees, but large enough to rival the height of the tallest bushes, the size of three tents combined. The chief kept his corona by the entrance. It was the skull of the great father of this tribe. The back of the skull had been broken off and the matter inside had been eaten so that his facade could fit over his son's head. This was the man who had conquered all the tribes of the bank, from the tree-dwellers to the ant-spitters, who stood taller than the trees and could break arrows with one throw of his glance. The piercing eyes of his skull and the plumes of parrot feathers pasted onto it greeted any passerby, a signal that the chief was there, and a warning not to come close. Nearer to the entrance were shells and pearls from the river, the shiniest and most polished of their kind.

The Silencer left me to enter. The chief kept his father's old spear, his father's old hair, in the same place as always, in a little pile near the corner where he slept. He was the only man who had mats on the floor made from the skins of the great cats he had slain. He lay in the centre of a mat on his side, staring at me, his manhood upwards as if it could detect the presence of a woman. He wasted no time in pulling me on top of him, pushing himself into me. His hands were on my breasts, my pelvis against his. He was scratching me. He was tugging my hair. He howled the way only a man of his hunger could howl. In the meantime, my eyes were dry, hard to keep open, and I felt hungry, in need of relieving my bowels.

He did not finish this time around. His bones cracked, and something about the way he bent his back made him seem tired. He gasped and heaved a bit, wanting to continue, but his body would not move. His hands pressed against the back of my ribs as he tried to stay inside, but whatever manhood he had was too tired to continue on his behalf. He was soggier than the fish paste served to children. How close I was to laughing at it all, at the least favourable of times. He stared so intently at me. The sight of my entire body was his.

We separated. He cursed himself, and stood up with effort. I looked at him and suddenly thought of the way a piece of wood mushed by the river falls apart. Afraid of what he could do when he was upset, I caressed his arm, crooned those soft words only men are silly enough to take seriously. He lay back by my side, but stared away from me. I took his hand into mine. He did not resist, and I tried to smile, but we were both thinking, *We shouldn't have done this...*

We spent the longest time lying side by side, saying nothing. He closed his eyes at certain times, as did I. How we both wanted to be apart at the furthest two points possible, and yet how we held each other's hand. There was nothing of love in the touch. There was something tired, something hurt, something afraid to let go. I closed my eyes and let my thoughts wander off. We all get a little foolish in the head after we do such things.

"Earlier on this very moon, I dreamt of you," I said. I did not tell him the dream where I had his son, a dream which would assuredly anger him more. Instead I told him about the dream I'd had a little before that one. "We were walking to where the sun began. The path was made of ants, and the ants gnawed at our bodies, but I never desisted. There was also an elder with red fruit shaped like balls of mud dangling from his ears. The serpent spoke to you. You listened to it and killed all the ants and me, and yet even in death I watched you. You cried because the elder, no matter how much you stabbed him with your spear, never faded away. Do you know what such a dream could mean?"

"It sounds like the same nonsense the spirits are making the shaman say. I think dreams are dreams, and nothing else."

You have returned to being the practical one, I thought. It was no different than our first night together, after the marriage ceremony. He held me like a raft of wood, he used my body as he pleased, and then he asked me to sleep in the tent for the concubines. *I am your first wife...* I told him. He responded, *Your place is with the concubines...* I stared away from the moonlight ringing against the animal rugs.

"How is the boy?"

"He is with his mother, resting," he said. I was right in my predictions. My daughter was too busy nursing and attending the newborn, and my husband could not go a single night without sex. I smiled to myself, imagining the grunting grimace she would make when she learned it was I who was spending this night with him. "Finally, the chief who will make the great cats kneel to man has been born."

I remembered the boy who had sat by me on the bank, called me mother, and asked for advice.

"That was the prediction meant for your first son, not for your second."

The chief made a gruff noise out of his nostrils.

"Do not speak of the other one again. We have a proper son in our midst. He shall be spoken of as the true chief. Mentioning that one — hah! He is practically a girl. Can you believe that I once again found him watching the river, playing with the mud and counting the fish like one of those idiots in the banished forest who speaks in tongues?"

"Perhaps he is studying the river for signs of what might happen next."

"That is the job of some lowly hunter, not a man who is meant to be a chief. He spends too much of his time chasing the monkeys, narrating their strategies as if it were some epic tale."

"Monkeys are very intelligent animals, my love."

"Well, then, are snakes?" asked the chief. "Or frogs? Or birds?"

"They are, in their own way," I said. "I believe I actually saw some birds—"

"Must you always contradict?" he asked. "Or is it age that has made you this disagreeable?"

He could have stabbed me with a spear and the pain would have not been so great. My hair had not yet greyed, nor had my breasts sagged, but our daughters were at the age I was when I married him. I was silent. I wanted nothing more than to sleep. *Why did I give this man so much...?* Without his crown of feathers, he was old, pathetic, a flame about to be extinguished. He was no longer ambitious or eager to please. Those traits had been passed on to his son, and now his skills were puffing his chest out and holding his face stiff.

"To think of how cursed we once were thanks to that girl," he sighed. He looked to the moon, and in that flash of a moment when he held down his face, held back his words and grew lost in his thoughts, I saw in his profile his father, himself, and his son. I was amazed. *The likeness between fathers and sons trickles through the face not by the bonds of blood, but through the passage of time...* "My true son has been born. A time of great peace will soon be upon us. This tribe will forget my failures and remember me for what I bestowed upon them — a worthy heir. Those accursed times are no more."

The chief grabbed me by the hair. He pulled me down to his face too quickly for me to be afraid. His eyes flashed with anger.

"If you had brought me a son, he would have never embarrassed us."

"I'm sorry," I wailed. He stood and pulled me up by the hair. My hair was short, but he lashed it like a whip.

"Nevertheless, you failed."

He flung me onto the rug. He spat on me like I was the corpse of his great enemy, then kicked dirt at my face. I curled into myself. Aching all over, driven to tears, I could no longer control the words I had hidden from him my entire life.

"I have loved you since the day I was born," I cried. Ever since the prophecy was relayed, I spent most of my youth imagining this tall and handsome man, gifting me with the servants of captured tribes, treating me with the compassion I rarely saw from my father, showering me with compliments. None of this happened, and I saw how he treated his other wives, and I grew bitter. Seeing the women around me, breastfeeding their children, cooking fish and turtle over a flame, thinking little about the relation between husband and wife but nurturing the lives of their children, I came to a conclusion. *Love is one of those things little children dream about, but something which no woman of age will experience...*

Then the chief married his youngest wife, and not even the river at its deepest of currents would be able to quench the flames of jealousy I felt when I saw the caress he gave to her upon the birth of that boy.

"Do you know how hard it is to see the love I dreamed of sharing not merely between my husband and another wife, but with my daughter? Do you know how painful it is to see from that love spring the male I could never provide? And, then, do you know how it shatters me, from the bones of my fingers to the bones of my ribs, to have to come here, service you for as long as you wish, and then have you hit me like this?"

He didn't speak. He reached for my hair, but pulled away like he was about to touch fire.

(The Chief's First Wife)

I was a papaya stripped of my peel,
stuck,
with something wet clinging to my bones,
us stuck in these positions,
as we had been for our entire lives.

God knew there were few souls,
in as much need of salvation, or divine love,
as his.

I stood.
He closed his legs and turned to his side.

God reminded me of the time,
not long ago,
when he came to seek my guidance,
not with his son, nor his wife,
but with his spilling heart alone.

It was not my place to speak.
Without a word
I excused myself,
and returned to the tent of the wives.

As he declared to me the words of his own son,
as he invited the boy to the church,
to give his own confessions,
I saw that this was more than a spat before a marriage,
they were in need of divine intervention.

I told myself never again.
This was not a promise meant
to be laughed at by the monkeys,
it was something said with utter faith.

I blessed them, with the deepest aches of my breath, knowing full well that I could help him. I agreed to take this long sojourn on my lunch break, en route to my friend's house, to solve the situation regarding his son's marriage. God knows I had kneeled by the side of many a former glue addict and palm wine drinker, and through my counselling, many of them had seen the light of the divine. If I could

(The Preacher)

mend their spirits, why couldn't I deal with a little boy and his future wife? God did whisper a warning that these two would be difficult to redirect. I wouldn't say harder times are befalling this village of mine. I have known it for a good three decades, almost four. People slaved away for a cent when I was growing up, and people slave away for cents these days. The problem was that I could count my ten fingers faster than I could count the families that knew the name of God. It is not that I discount the gods of others. I myself was giving sacrifices to the lightning and the land until I was in my twenties. Let them be known as gods. Let them be known as our saviours. We are all tied down to this earth due to our higher beings, and they guide us to do good. But I have done missionary work for a good thirteen years now, and let me say this. I have traveled from the end of the creek to the hills on the other side of the cow estate. I have counted almost every one of the twenty-three mud huts that one encounters on these fields. I myself live in the only government housing complex in a ten-kilometre radius. I could say, strolling on this trail, passing by men and women who knew my family, who knew what I do, that the boys and girls under the age of twenty knew more about television characters than stories from the teachings, and that each and every person over the age of twenty was a proud and shameless sinner.

The best example of that trend was walking far from my line of vision. He did not hide the fact that he was taking a girl nearly half his age to the creek any more than he hid the tattoo of the flaming skull on his right shoulder. He had a wife who often took trips to town to get her hair cut and buy cosmetics, like all of the women. She was a religious girl, God bless her. She came to church almost every three days, crying her spirit out for the sake of a man who had the most violent of pornography on his phone. How she had never come to realise she was being cheated on, I will never know. God knows that I have called the police on this man a handful of times, but they never did a thing. The village was too far to drive out to for the sake of something that, unless you were willing to give them an extra something, was not a crime in their eyes.

The carpenter was not passing me, nor were any of his family members. God knows that his store was one of the last ones on the paved road before the road led into wilderness, leaving it a motorcycle drive away and not a walk, unless he wanted to bake his hair straight in the heat and humidity. I do not think I have ever seen him leave his station for work. He is that hard-working. As I was reaching the end of the trail and turning onto one of the set of trails that led to various huts, the curvier one to my far left inevitably leading to the housing complex, the woman who was carrying logs on her head on her way to her own home remembered who I was and blessed God. It was something the carpenter did often. I never saw his family at church. I never saw his family pray. They have one of the biggest houses in the area, the second biggest after the cow estate. I believe it to be one of his own constructions. How strange it was, to see these mud huts that have been used for centuries by people oblivious to history, and then a cottage of two storeys on the far-flung side, modelled after some style of cottage house from a continent far, far away. I imagine God was testing him in a more nuanced manner. In his case, it was a matter of how much he thought of himself and yet how little he thought for the sake of an impoverished community.

Enough about them. I had left my abode of worship, not in fact to enter my proper abode, but because I had been asked to solve a problem by a man who was dearer to me than my actual brothers. We were to meet with the girl in question and his son at his place within the hour. I could see her in clear view. There was a field carved out of the dust by the boys for the sake of their games. Because it was a weekend, it was full with all the boys of the village in a football match, and the one girl who was crossing their way to play with them. All of these boys had problems. One of them sat by the side of the field and played video games on his phone all day, and was failing school. Then there were the twins. They liked to kick the ball around, but they also had their phones out constantly, taking videos of anything and everything and putting them on the internet, whether it be a harmless ball game or a fight between their parents. God knows I had sermons for each and every one of them, but for today I was here to see the milkmaid. She was around the age of sixteen, and wore an orange dress that had belonged to her mother and her grandmother before her, its diamond sequins long since chipped away. I had seen her earlier in the distance. She had been balancing her pail over her head and delivering milk to some of the women who were outside the housing complex, cooking. She was known for two things in our village.

The first was related more to her family and less to her. Her father was one of the worst hedonists to exist in a hundred-kilometre radius. He was so rich off the milk of his cows that he had a literal harem of village girls. Most of them got pregnant and were forced to abort. I know this because many of them sought my help and advice. The preacher who had helped me find God told me that many of the young women had committed suicide due to the awareness of their sins, while others had to leave town. Only one kept her child, and she became the milkmaid. This mother committed suicide later on. Her father is also dead. There remain many mysteries as to how he died. I think anyone of even mediocre intelligence could spot certain abrasions on his body and a weakness to his gait. Nevertheless, he went out at every minute of every day, selling milk no one wanted to buy, but had to buy, because it was the only source of milk, unless they wanted to drive ten kilometres to town.

As an orphan, and one that was raised poorly, the milkmaid was exempt from certain judgments. I am sure a lot of people wanted her to marry into their families, not only because of the value of her cows, but because she simply needed a family. God knows I invited her to church every time she delivered milk to our house, because I wanted her to know community, and I believed that she deserved it. She was the only person I knew who had rebuffed my invitations by openly telling me that God does not exist. She said it in a joking way — she would pretend to be a cartoon character or an oracle summoning spells — but at some point, she had to say, quite brashly, that she could never believe in a God. During these exchanges, my wife would make conversation with the girl, trying to draw her out. Once she took the opportunity to caution the milkmaid about how she dressed. While the young woman could always be seen in the only dress she owned, it was tearing in all the wrong places as she grew into her breasts and her hips.

The scene that was unfolding before me showed how little she cared. She was crossing the same path that I had been crossing. She would often stop during her rounds and play a bit of football with the boys, and thus when they saw her, without thinking, they passed her the ball. The milkmaid must have forgotten that she had a giant pail of milk on her head. She ran over and kicked it with such abandon that the pail fell and spilled milk all over her entire dress and body. Certainly, it would dry up in this heat, and she probably had enough milk at home to spare. Yet, as the boys surrounded her, an engaged woman, soon to be married, she was covered from head to toe in a layer of milk. She was not wearing a bra. She was not wearing underwear. The entire outline of her body was visible to every boy on the football field. She did not make any effort to cover herself. She did not hide herself away. She did not take a look even to her right, to notice one of the twins crouching a bit away from her, recording her debauchery on his phone. She simply laughed, said something inaudible from this distance, and played football with the boys.

In this sense, I clearly saw what my friend and his son were bemoaning. God knows that I closed my eyes, said a prayer for her, and then said another prayer, when she went to a nearby bucket used to feed the goats, stripped down, and washed her dress in the water, with no regard for the temptation such behavior would inspire in front of the teenage boys. In such a circumstance, I could do nothing more than pray. Was it a blessing or a curse that the ball came this way, with my eyes closed and my mind deep in meditation, and whacked my nose with all the strength of a brick? They say that God works in mysterious ways. While I blew the blood out with the snot, the one who came to retrieve this ball was in fact the milkmaid. I grabbed the ball before she could lay her hands on it.

"I have come — *achoo!* — to see you," I told her between sneezes, as my nose was still suffering from the blow.

"Do you want milk?" she asked me.

"Nothing of that sort," I said. I thought she was motioning to take the ball from me, but her gestures became clear when she pulled out a handkerchief from some part of her dress. I put my hand to my heart and refused. As God would say, we must outdo one another in compassion. "Thank you, my child." I put out my palms to say a blessing, but she was not kneeling or putting her hands in prayer stance. "We must leave, my child. God has a test for you that I must enact." The milkmaid was putting her hands in a prayer stance, but with an exaggerated smile, and she had scrunched up her eyes. "So, sorry, very sorry, but I have game! Good, good, bye!" Then she ran off.

Dare I say it, the strands of sunlight enveloped her dress with an almost exalted glow, which was ruined by the way she was tipping her toes together and pressing her hands. What was stranger yet was how the boys who were waiting for the ball no longer seemed to care. They were running out to her in this strange posture, as if this were the new game they were going to play. There was this famous author my father loved who was quoted as saying that all of life was a stage, and it was common to see the youngsters, educated by television serials from all of the continents, pretend they were somewhere else. Damn them all. I had a mission to fulfil. God granted me with the exact sentence to stop her in her tracks.

"The one who has contacted me is none other than your fiancé. I think it would be in your best interest to come with me."

I thought the milkmaid was marching up to her friends because she was going to ignore me. My friend wouldn't have enlisted me in this intervention had the young woman not been a difficult soul. But she did not remain with the boys. She stole the ball from my hands only to kick it to them, and then she took her pail, flung it on top of her head, and with one hand at the rim and the other by her waist, she asked, "So, what does Klickety Klack want?" "Klickety Klack?" I asked we walked away from the field together and back in the direction of the mud huts. She responded, "Klickety Klack has shoes that are spick and spack, he drives a bike 'cuz he knows he's whack." She was laughing to herself. "There's this thing called rap, and the way I am into ball, my fiancé is really into it. Don't tell his father this, but it's one of his dreams to get into music. I mean, he's seventeen, and he tells me something else about his goals almost every day. Just a month ago, we got into one of these series you see on the TV, and he liked the way some of the vampires looked. Do you know what vampires are? A lot of the old folk don't know, so it's totally normal if you don't. I usually tell them vampires are like those ghosts we have in our folklore, but they suck blood and the only animal form they take is like a bat. So, he loves the way vampires look, and he said he wanted to get to one of these cities and become a graphic designer so he can draw vampires and zombies and all of these foreign monster things and get paid for it. Maybe that's why he's making you bring me to his house, so he can practice drawing a zombie."

That wasn't the reason we were walking towards his father's hut in the least. I hadn't been responding because I couldn't understand eighty percent of what she was referring to — "zombies," "vampires," and other beasts were all new to me — but I gathered that she wanted me to pose as something, and God's plan was much greater than that. The heat was also quite testing. Towards the hour of one, the sun was at its peak, and the path between the trail and the creek afforded us little shade. We were as exposed to the sun as the wild grass and the goats. The milkmaid saw I was in need of a drink. She took the small copper cup out of her pail and served me from the portion of milk that hadn't spilled, all the while balancing it on her head and walking. She carried on while I drank, "The point is, he has a lot of dreams, and I do too. Once we both turn eighteen, we're getting out of here and becoming the people we want to be." She kicked the air as if there was a ball there, and this time, no milk was spilling.

We were soon outside of their hut. It was one of the huts near the creek, and it showed. The walls had a suppleness to them from all the moisture in the air, and straw was not falling out of the room. My friend saw that we had arrived. He came outside to greet me, but said nothing to the girl who had been arranged for the last half-year to be his son's bride. He asked us to come inside and offered us sugar cane juice. Inside the hut, the ants scurried from one cot to another, picking up pieces of biscuit and twigs. I recognised the boy who had come to confess. He used his cot as a chair, a resting place for his flute, and a study, with books on subjects ranging from biology to geometry and beyond. God knows I have met with the most eccentric of characters to be seen in a village as small as this one, but when elders meet with youngsters, it is common for the elders to do all of the talking and for the youngsters to sit quietly and await their judgment. The milkmaid had put her pail outside and was coming up to her fiancé with her fist clapping against her hand and with her lips pushed out. "What up, Klick?" she said. I had never seen someone below the age of eighteen, particularly a girl, greet a man in such a bizarre way. I felt that this boy, who was supposed to be on good terms with her, was also acting as if it wasn't correct. He clicked his tongue, and he looked away. I was of the feeling that he had something to say but did not want to say it. There are those whom God emboldens and those whom He doesn't. At that moment, it was his father, or my friend, who was responding, and with yelling. "What is she doing? Get your hands off my son! Go over there, now." He turned to face me. "Didn't you tell her yet?" Both his son and I stood up and in between the two. "Calm yourself," I said. "Father dearest, please, wait," was what his son said, but he didn't look at his fiancée, and his words seemed to stick in his throat. The milkmaid stood in the middle of it all, not moving, then turned to her betrothed. "What are you saying? You were going to tell me, what?" Her voice was quivering and her big, round eyes were beginning to mist over.

"Let us begin," I said. I took the milkmaid, and guided her by the elbow onto the cot. The boy and his father sat opposite us. "Dear God, oh wondrous God." I opened my eyes momentarily to make sure they were all repeating. "Dear God, oh wondrous God," said the father and his boy, but not the milkmaid. I nudged her to speak up. She closed her eyes and spoke up, "Dear God, oh wondrous God." Something in her tone bothered me. *That better not have been an imitation of me.* I pressed on. "Dear God, oh wondrous God, we have the son of my dear friend, one of the most successful men our village has known, a man who twenty years ago went all the way to the city in a bull cart to sell cassavas, beet roots, and plantains, and now has enough money to ship them in his own lorry." My friend was beaming while he reached for my hand. I pressed it firmly against mine, thanked God silently for his success, and returned to the previous matter. "His son is as talented at playing the flute as he capable of scoring well in math and science. He will make a fine engineer indeed. He was to marry our village milkmaid. We see now that this marriage was not meant to be in your plan."

"What?" interrupted the milkmaid. She looked at me, then fixed her eyes on her fiancé. "What do you mean you're no longer marrying me? What's happening here?" When no one spoke, I addressed her, saying, "I think we can all see that God has a plan better for both you and he—" but the son said, "I think we need to talk about this later." The milkmaid was in no listening mood. She stood up, shouted, "You lady's finger!" and punched him in the chin. The boy tried to punch back but she weaved backwards and he missed. He lunged at her again but I grabbed him and pulled him away. Meanwhile, the boy's father had grabbed the milkmaid and was pushing her out of the hut, shouting "Get out of here, vile girl!" Once outside, he shouted to her, "You never come back." His son followed them outside and was holding his cheek and moving his jaw around while the muscles of her left arm bulged and threatened the air. "Aw'you a whittle cwy baby? Can't take a whittle swap from a girl? Fine. Like I should marry a man who would have to ask me to open his jars." My friend shouted, "Get out, now." Just as the milkmaid finally turned and started to walk away, the son yelled after her,

"I'm glad the carpenter's daughter told me the truth about you. Go to the men who gave you those blotches, you whore!" The milkmaid turned and stared at him, her mouth hanging wide open, eyes wide as saucers. She watched the boy turn and go inside, then buried her face in her hands and walked away.

When the milkmaid was out of sight and we were all back inside the hut, my friend turned to me and said, "Thank you for being willing to help. It is not what a normal preacher would do."

"No, no," I responded. "Thank you, for coming to visit me, for praying to God, for confiding in me." My friend offered me money, but I accepted the payment in the form of a hug. I told the boy, "You no longer have to worry about her. You can go back to playing your flute." His father reminded him, "Your flute lesson is in two hours and ten minutes, remember?" The boy mouthed, "Two hours and ten minutes," and his father pinched him on the shoulder. God knows I have seen many who grew up to have double lives, but this boy held his flute with much rigour.

I would like to say that this was the last that I thought about the milkmaid for this day. I certainly had the problems of other devout men and women to balance in my mind, and it was long past my lunchtime. I went towards the exterior of the housing complex, and I saw my wife, in her group of friends sitting on a circle outside, their saucepans balanced against the earth by one brick, their cooking finished. She grinned at me, with only three teeth left in her smile. I had the habit of eating in my home garments. I told her, "I will come eat, let me change first." My wife was so busy with her friends that she never went inside of the house. It was on the ground floor of the housing complex, one room that had a television and a cot for our thirteen-year-old son, and our room, which had its own cot, and some dressers, and a bookshelf for my readings. Normally, when I had to open the door, I spent much time fumbling for my keys, and there were two or three bolts that had to be unlocked. My wife had chosen to not lock up this one time.

It was for this reason that I snapped open the door with ease, and I encountered my son, sprawled out on his cot, his one hand pressing his phone against his face, his other hand deep into his groin, his entire manhood out for me to see. He was quick to hide it back into his pants, but I was quicker. I slapped his phone out of his hand, I yelled some words at him I cannot recall. I grabbed his phone with the intention of giving it back to him. He was telling me not to touch it, begging, in fact. I happened to take the shortest of glimpses to notice whose picture he was touching himself to. It was a picture of none other than the milkmaid.

"Who is this?" I asked, despite knowing very well who it was. My son did not answer. I stared at the image long enough for an entire gospel song to have been sung. It was of the girl I had seen an hour earlier, stained with milk, washing herself in a bucket, sent to my son by those twins, or one of his friends. In all that wetness, the shape of her breasts and her curves was almost transparent. It was literally transparent in certain areas due to the rips in her dress. I threw the phone at the wall. It was one of these cheap pre-smart phones which easily shattered all over the place. My son was shielding his head with his hands as if he were expecting to be hit in a similar way.

He must have been surprised when I sat down by him and stared at the ceiling.

God was testing me. A few months ago, when my son was a good fifteen minutes late to lunch, I decided to look around for him. I happened to hear some strange noises by the outhouse. It was the wild moaning which accompanied ejaculation, and then the suspirations of a minute of rest. My wife asked me what had happened. I did not have the peace of mind to answer. I immediately stood to myself and prayed. I asked God why he brought temptation into the mind of a man who was raised by a man and woman who knew how to control themselves. I asked God whether this was something all men inevitably did, or was it something to be looked down upon, something which encouraged sin. I was not able to reach a conclusion when he came to eat, and I was not able to reach a conclusion when I caught him again. I talked to him instead over something I knew was wrong.

I asked my son, "Where did you get this photo from?" He said, "It wasn't something I took. It was something my friend sent me, I swear." God does not discriminate between the photos one takes and those one receives. I said, "But, it is a photo that you knew was wrong to take. She clearly did not give her consent. What would you do if someone took your photo like this?" My son's response was "I don't know," but I had more to say. "What would you do if you knew someone was touching themselves the way you were touching yourself, to a photo of yourself walking, or studying?" My son shouted, "I don't know!" and started to cry. Only God would know if they were the genuine tears of someone who had realised his perversity, or if he was doing what all toddlers did in order to sway their parents.

Regardless of the answer, there was only one thing I knew was right to be done. I took his palm, the one which had not touched himself, and we prayed.

"Dear God, oh wondrous God," I said. He said, "Dear God, oh wondrous God."

"I am sorry with all of my heart about what I did."

"I am sorry with all of my heart about what I did."

"I am not meant to make little girls my playthings."

"I am not meant to make little girls my playthings."

"Women are meant to be respected, for from each and every woman comes children, from each and every woman comes another mother or father, and when I do as I did, I am making them into something they are not."

"Father, I don't want to say something like that."

"You are going to say it, and you are going to say it well."

"Women are meant to be respected. Women make children, and some woman will someday become a mother, and when I do things like that, I will make them feel bad."

"Good boy," I said. I rubbed his head with my other hand because he had meant it. "God will forgive all sins, for he loves me, and he will take me on the righteous path. Amen." My son sat up from his little space on his cot and wiped his eyes with his arm, and said, "Amen." I wanted to wrap my own arm around him, but I found it hard. We watched the termites file through a crack in our wall.

God decided that our conversation needed change. My son told me he needed better clothes for school. I told him that no matter how tattered the tie got, a uniform was a uniform, and a preacher's salary was meagre. We didn't have the money to get him clothes every single year. I asked what he was studying these days. He said he had a geography test tomorrow. I asked him randomly if it got cold enough in other parts of the world that the dirt froze over. He told me that dirt does not freeze. We spent a good minute laughing at my mistake.

Relations

Pitter-patter, crick-crunch, amongst the leaves. After the events of the previous moon, the chief's son came to my tent and wanted a word with me. He kneeled to the ground outside and tapped his chest twice, then held his hands there for another beat. It was a greeting to a respected elder. Monkeys were rustling in the finger trees as the wind blew the roof twigs flat. I was about to invite him in when I noticed a dark spirit in the shadows — a hovering figure stabbed with arrows, with two seething holes where its eyes should have been and a grasping hand. I took one step outside of my tent, kneeled in the moss, and stared into the two stains in the voids of its eyes. I threw one of the snakeheads at it and some of the powder made from the bark of the neighbouring trees. I danced to this stranger and chanted to it and it alone.

"It is you again! This time, do not tease me. Who is it that has come to attack our tribe? Did a handful of the tree-dwellers survive? No, they are peaceful, unlike the flame-worshippers. But, the flame-worshippers along with the ant-spitters were completely decimated. Who could have survived? Eat from the sacred seeds and tell me!"

The spirit was leaving. Cracked embers of darkness, thrust into the wind, cinders and ashes. My vision returned to this world, and I could see that the fire outside my hut was extinguished, and that some twigs from the roof of my hut had fallen onto the silt. I knew the difference between when a spirit intervened and when a human responded. Panting, collapsed shoulders, dust stains alongside the legs were all signs that a person was present. The chief's son had jumped up and kicked all the dirt and the leaves.

"Not even the infants are scared when the spirits descend," I said.

"I'm so sorry," apologised the chief's son. "I'm so, so sorry!"

One of the men who lived in the tent next to mine was approaching. He patted clawed hands towards his chest and bared his teeth. A face made to scare off monkeys, to challenge a thief, to strip down a wife.

He turned to the chief's son and stared him down. "Stupid boy, what are you doing? Do you know whose hut you are next to?" He extended his hand towards me. "This is the shaman's hut, not the poking place of some girl you want to stick yourself into."

This man was in no position to speak to any of the chief's family in such a way. A proper son of the chief would have gutted him with his spear and ended it at that. This boy bent by the fireplace, his head in his hands, making the wild screeches of a pregnant great cat.

"I am in the middle of work," I told him, though I quickly realised that that might be hard for anyone to believe. Most of the snakeheads or turtle claws or bones around the fireplace were left over from previous ceremonies. None of the drummers had been summoned for a possession. Not a single person was visiting me for an infection that needed healing or for the clarification of a vision. An oddity, I realised then. The sacred drink which ought to be drunk once in a lifetime ought to have been hidden behind mounds of shells and herbs, but it was standing there in the open between the fireplace and the entry to my hut. I hid it inside my hut and came back outside to find the chief's son rehearsing something to himself.

When he saw me, he stood up, kept his arms straight, and said out loud what he'd been mouthing: "I came here on behalf of my father. He is quite concerned about your prophecy, and would like to have a proper audience with you concerning it."

"Come back later," I said. A spirit standing by the beam of my hut whispered into my ear that it was a lie.

"But ... but ... my father wanted me to talk to you. He really, really did." The boy's legs were shaking. One of the animal skins held in place by one of my husband's spears fell down. The chief's son was about to pick it up and disturb another spear when I grabbed his arm and pulled him away.

"You will get nowhere in life if you act like this," I said. I took both of my palms and rubbed them over his cheeks. He looked away. They always do. My face is powdered black like a nightmare, and it is only when the spirits come inside of me that my eyes look alive.

"I know, I know," he said. The unsettled hands, the bit lip, the perked ears. He was waiting for me to tell him his father was wrong, that all fathers were tough on their sons, and that what I saw in him was greatness, if only he could learn how to channel that energy for himself. These were all things I did think, but I saw no purpose in saying them to see his eyes beam for once.

Whatever he had come to glean from me was not to be given. A man was shouting for the shaman in the finger trees, his voice growing louder as he sprinted into the clear.

"Shaman, come," he said. "You must see this."

Before I reached the periphery of the hut, he was already standing under the hanging branches of a nearby tree, and with company. Four men were walking between the finger trees and the moss, carrying something between them. The shape was that of an ant-spitter, its corpse the colour of silt, snakeskins wrapped around its feet, blue thatch covering the legs, red and white bark checkered over the chest. It lived in something other than its skin. Another spirit appeared next to my hut. I asked her if she knew what the creature was. She said she had never seen anything like it. Neither, of course, had the wives harvesting papayas, the boys playing under the roots of the walking trees, the men hooting at the monkeys and hunting with their spears. A dozen of them crowded around the line of four men.

"Stop this milling around," said one of the warriors who was holding this thatched man. "We are still en route to the chief's hut."

Just as the chief's son and I were both about to speak, a group of men came running along the path from the north and pushed us into each other, then crashed into the four warriors. As the warriors lost their grip on the ant-spitter, it fell and smashed into a log and rolled onto its belly. The arrows stuck out of its back like the feathers of a parrot.

"I remember a story of one of these from my grandfather," one of the men said.

"What did your grandfather say?"

"Stop shoving! Stop shoving!" said another man. Every man and boy and woman wanted to touch the thatch on his skin.

"He said that—"

"Mommy, I'm hungry."

"—and that they eat not turtle, not papaya, but the silt itself—"

"Hey, look what he's got!"

The group looked down to see a piece of metal cut in the shape of a finger, sharper than an arrow, heavier than a spear. One of the men ripped it off him.

"—they are known for mating with the great cats and thus they also grow fur—"

The man who had snapped off the metal object began to swing it around widely and the tip caught the arm of another man, breaking the skin. Their own fight began.

"What is this, too?"

The red and white skin sloughed off the body and lay on the ground. A boy in the crowd moved forward and pushed the ant-spitter over so that he was lying on his arrows. Two nipples, a fat stomach, a belly button, facing sky. The boy picked up the red and white skin and flapped it against his mother and friends. He was also chased by some of the men. The four warriors tried to fight for the body they had found. They had to fight. The other men were tearing it apart. I turned to the chief's son.

"Will you not say anything to control your men?"

He looked down at his fingernails and said nothing. This was the boy who was divined to tame the great cats with one stare, yet he could not control one small crowd. I was the only woman of power nearby. I was about to assert myself when the boy did in fact bellow something.

"Hey! Hey! That body is meant for the chief and his family first!"

No one listened. The chief's son was leaving.

"I must go to tell my father about this."

I could not help but take his hand.

"Don't think you are the cause of all of this tribe's problems. The only people who blame you are the ones who are weak."

The chief's son kept a firm grip on my hand until I finally shook it off and told him that I needed to see the ant-spitter's body. As I did so, he looked up at me and spoke.

"I promise I will make you proud. I will find a way to be chief, I promise."

I was tempted to encourage him. There was no law that said a man who cried at circumcision could not be chief, and he was the first son of the chief who was destined to make the great cats bow and the moon meet the sun. The prophecies spoke nothing of even the birth of a second son. Yet, at the rate the infant was learning to express himself, he would master speech and weaponry quickly as well. I wondered if one son was destined to be the chief but the other would be more apt at being chief. It would certainly create a conflict once the chief was to die. The spirits had warned me a few moons ago that it might be soon.

I had little time to reflect on any of this. Someone had already suspended the thatched man's red and white skin between the wooden beams of a hut near the papaya plants.

"Hey! Hey!" I yelled. "Do not tamper with that body. I am the shaman of this tribe. Let me see!"

I must have spoken with the voice and mannerisms of a demon. The men and women and children who were nearby stared at me as they cleared a line to the body. Meanwhile, the four warriors saw this as a chance to shove themselves back into prominence as well. The thatched man no longer had any thatch on his body. He was as bare-skinned as any man or woman of this tribe. Two ears, two eyes, one nose. This confirmed he was a human.

I did not see any more. The spirit was possessing me, and I was beginning to lose consciousness. The arrow in his demon neck dripped blood, while the eyes took the shape of two flames, and a hand strangled me to the ground. Words spilled from my mouth.

"The end of days is near. The end of days is near. The red tree's feet will fall to new men. The spirits will attack from inside out. Arrows will strike our kin. They are coming, they are coming! They will kill our chief. They will eat our flesh. The water will wash our bones clean. The land will belong to them. The end, the end! It is coming, our end!"

When I woke to myself, I was outside my hut, my head in the lap of my husband, and the words this spirit had told me were ringing. The body of the ant-spitter was gone. Blood seeped into the twigs, pieces of muscle were sutured into the moss, and a torn finger lay on my snakeskins. I assumed parts of the thatched man were eaten. I rested further into the belly of my loved one. It was rare that he did not stand by the side of the chief.

"Did the chief come?" I asked.

"Mhm."

"And what did he say?"

He was as silent as his pet name. Words said little between the two of us in the first place. I sat up and stared into his eyes. They were direct and demanding in concern for my health over anything else. I told him first.

"Only one night ago I was taken by a bad spirit, right in the middle of the birthing ceremony for our chief's second son. The spirit spoke to me until the moon became the sun. I believe you were at my side during his visit, but I am not sure."

"Mhm," which I took as a sign to continue.

"This same spirit has visited me once more, and he showed me something else. I only had to see the thatched man's body once to imagine thousands of them at the foot of our land. The waters were rising. The body of the chief lay dead on the silt. I cannot tell him any of this, for I do not know how he will react."

My loved one said no "Mhm," which I took to mean I was right.

"I am not in control of what has been channeled through me. Whatever was said has been said. It is up to fate to decide what comes next."

My body was shaking the entire time I spoke, and I felt something worse than a demon lodged deep in my chest. I picked myself up. I launched into another little dance and asked once more for the spirit to come. I could do little afterwards other than think of my loved ones. A sweaty body, a cooing sound, skin soft as the flesh around a papaya's seeds.

"I am disturbed," I said. "We won't be able to fight against the thatched men. We will be finished. We need to leave, but where would we go? What land is there that exists beyond the jungles and the rivers? I need to advise the chief to seek the ends of the earth. No, you go and talk to him. I need to go see my sister."

I stared into his eyes so deeply and for so long that it was no longer me who was staring at him at all. His stare did not waver. He took his palms and rubbed my cheeks, pushing his face against mine, and uttered another "Mhm."

I went alone. My sister's hut was lodged much further in the jungle, at least twenty huts from ours. Such was the price of being the shaman; I had to live near the chief and his huts in case my services were needed. The path to these huts itself was tame. Many of the trees had been cleared out except for the thick ones with trunks the size of three men. Those trees scattered their root-legs on both sides of the path and sheltered the bushes from our hands. The mud had been caked by the heat and thudded against the feet. I kicked away some of the sticks on the ground and avoided the shoots that had thorns. Between the trees I could hear the laughter of children.

The oldest of my sister's wifes-in-law was awake but outside the family hut, bashing a turtle against a rock so that she might cook its insides later. That woman never stopped complaining about how hard it was to live since she twisted her ankle. My sister told me the woman asked the same questions over and over again: "Can you believe I have to take care of ten children in this pain? Why do none of you take care of me? Don't you remember the times when family happily came to your aid?" She put down the dead turtle and bowed her face into the silt. Then, she leaned up, put both of her palms to her chest, and pursed her lips. I kissed my palm and touched it to her forehead.

My sister was inside the hut, sleeping, along with eight of her children and her husband's other wives.

Some straw had fallen out of the roof and had allowed the heat of the sun to filter into the shadows. I stared at the family from outside the hut, catching glimpses of their faces and bodies. I was glad to see my sister asleep. It was hard to rest in this area. It was far from the river and the other huts. Monkeys often pillaged fruits and arrows and even the bones of the deceased from inside. The men often had to stay awake at night to guard against the great cats.

"Is that you?"

The spirits often spoke in whispered tones. It was more of a gust that nicked at the ear than a voice. And yet, I had grown so unaccustomed to hearing my sister that my neck shivered straight and my hand reached for one of my herbs around my neck. My body's instinct was to counter this spirit with a curse. I was not, however, in the midst of a ceremony or summoning.

"What are you doing?" My sister shouted from across the other wives. One or two opened their eyes and stirred, while others found another position and slept on. The baby being held by my sister, my nephew, was quite disturbed. He wailed and thrashed more than the branches stirred amid the river's toss.

"I did not mean to do him any harm," I said.

"I know," my sister said, her voice adjusted once more to a whisper. She shushed her child against her breast and caved her entire body towards the log holding the roof above. I moved myself towards the other side of the hut and let the breeze of the open space calm my shoulders. "It has been long since you have come. What has made you return?"

I could have said it was because the end of our tribe was near. I could have said I did not know for how many more moons and suns I would be able to see them.

"I wanted to see my nephew," I did say. "He is the closest thing I have to a son."

"I am sure," my sister yawned. She pushed the baby into my arms, lay back down next to her husband's wives, and shut her eyes as if I had not even come.

I held the firm weight of the child against my chest. His long body draped over my shoulder, and I patted him along the back. I hushed him to be quiet and kept him as far away from my face and my body as possible. I had the bones of people and turtles and fish in a garland around my waist, and the spirits had left me bald. Somehow, the child settled. He began to cuddle into the warmth of my arms. I imagined myself as my sister. I thought of this child feeding from my breast. I thought of him falling before he stood, crawling before he could walk. I thought of him having wives, children. I thought of how I would die, how he would die, how life moved on.

"Please," said my sister, from the place where she lay. "If you want to take care of him, I will sleep alone in the shaman's tent. I am more than happy to switch places."

I was not going to tell her about the tragedy soon to strike our tribe. I was not going to tell her that she and her boy would soon have to move. I wanted to hold this boy for as long as I was able to. I held the boy close to my breast and said, "Sure."

She stood up from her space in the den with her eyes still shut.

"Really? Would you be willing to sacrifice your calling for a boy who is not even yours?"

(The Shaman)

For a boy that coos at me and giggles
when I touch my nose against his?

It was like, duh.

For a boy that was my family, my blood,
the son I never had?

I would get on my knees,
pull those cassavas and make my hips sweat.
I might even kiss a damn goat.
I would do anything for a sweetie
who gave me attention and affection
even when I was shameless and not cute.

"I would sacrifice my life and a thousand more."

It wasn't like I was anywhere near this man of mine,
being at the carpenter's house, his daughter throwing some
shindig or soirée, around all of these little girls too young
to be called bitches, though they were totally dressed for it,
putting on the wigs and dresses some girl had bought last
time she was in the city and pretending to be from
somewhere they weren't, but they invented phones for a
reason, and it wasn't so that people who lived in the
middle of these nowhere villages could set up fake call
centres and scam people in faraway countries. By the way,

(Milker)

I had a cousin who totally did that, running it from the family hut. Place looked more like a science lab than a home. Not that I have seen a science lab; I don't think they have many of them in the capital, but I have seen them in photos and TV shows, so I had about as much knowledge of them as that sixteen-year-old who put so much pink makeup on her skin that it looked like mud cracking in the heat, or the twelve-year-old who was wearing a miniskirt over the folds of her dress. There was nothing cute about lumpy denim over purple and black dress fabric, which was why one of the two girls lying on cots on the floor was smirking at her, and then at me, and was like, "Don't pay the poor thing any attention," with a smug wink. I was too distracted by the ants to notice what the girls were saying. Someone had dropped a chicken bone, and the ants were coming in by the thousands, trailing from a crack in the wall over to the bone, turning it into a writhing black form. Where was a broom when you needed one?

And then, someone had to interrupt my phone time by asking me to teach her how to walk in heels. The wooden planks we were walking over were budging more than her face. I was like, "I'm busy right now, and why are you asking a boy to teach you to walk in heels when there are so many girls practising right in front of you?" I pointed to the line of girls strutting along a makeshift catwalk between the cots and the door frame, the clacking of their footsteps making the tables and chairs creak and shake. She was like, "Because I saw you walk the last time we were invited to the carpenter's house, and you were way better at it than they were." I was like, "Don't say that too loud." I know I was young, but last time, I had a bit of the palm wine that the carpenter's daughter had stolen from her father, so I was doing all sorts of things I wouldn't have done on a normal day. I was like, "Go ask someone else. I said I'm busy," and made it a point to look at my phone, when all I really wanted was more of that palm wine that she wasn't able to steal this time around. Palm wine was good at making you forget that although cell phone technology had finally arrived in in the village, this was still a place where most folk did their laundry at the creek and spent part of every day praying to their God — and that those same nice folks would happily shoot you like a diseased goat if you were a boy wearing lipstick.

Anyways, I wasn't staying here too long, and I was going to live my life the way all those fabulous darlings like me got to style rich girls in big cities or make love to each other, in their beds, shirts off, quite openly. It was from one of these shows that I found out about the gay dating app thing, and it was from that thing that I found the only other guy in a ten-kilometre radius, just one week ago, and we were talking to each other every damn day. I was going to his mobile store during his lunch break and giving him everything his wife couldn't. I leaned against the wall next to a black-and-white portrait of the carpenter's mother, at an angle where no one could see the app I was using to send him all of those messages. The weird thing is, he wasn't answering. Otherwise I would have been with him instead of here at this house. Because no one wants to see all these local girls pretending to be foreigners, hunching their shoulders, reading gossip magazines for tips on how to be bitchier, faking bad accents, and putting their dresses and wigs on all wrong. Not even me.

The house was a mess. Plates of food sat on the tables, half-eaten and covered in flies. The carpenter's wife had delivered lunch to us and then gone out to eat with her friends, leaving that part of the house looking like a disaster zone. I was about to start cleaning it up when the girl with the too-big forehead came running over to me. She was like, "Darling, what do you think of this makeup?" Honestly, girl had so much powder on she was struggling to breathe, but she was pulling my hand so hard that my only option was to lie. "I love it," I said, and I twirled her by the hand and caught her. My phone vibrated, and I dropped her, which I know was totally rude and unbecoming of me, and it wasn't worth it because it was a voice message from my mother, who still didn't know how to use her phone, so half of the time her voice messages are just random recordings of static or bleating goats. Forehead girl was obviously pissed, and went back to her side of the cot, clown mascara all over her face, back hunched, staring at the bush and fence outside the door.

I had my own things to stare at, but none of them were in front of me. I had to imagine it instead — his hard, thick dick, waiting for someone to squeeze it, and then the way he put his hands around my belly, his breath all over my neck, the way he was good at thrusting. The one thing I didn't like about his light-chocolate eyes was that he could smile at me, he could say a pretty thing, but he could never make his looks at me come alive. Don't get me started on how bad he was when it came to talking, either. Maybe it would be better when he finally saved up enough money to got us out abroad, where we could marry, do all the fun things we want, so on.

I was getting too hot and bothered, so I picked up some of the chicken bones that were still lying around, put them on their plates, and went out to wash them. The good thing about cleaning was that it made it easier to hover over these fifteen girls on the cots and stare at them. One of them was stroking her scalp, dandruff snowing everywhere. Another was outside, washing sheep dung off her feet. Another was making her naturally shiny hair gleam by correctly applying makeup to her cheeks. She twirled in front of the others while her friend read a fashion magazine, keeping her mouth closed to hide her bad teeth. How could I forget the day's star, the carpenter's daughter, sitting by the horse-faced girl, handing out the wigs from a bag, wearing one of those blonde wigs, making a kissy face into her mirror, striking a pose. The girl handing out the wigs was like, "Lookin' good, honey," and I totally agreed. With her wig on, you could tell she was a girl. Without it, and without makeup, she was like a bush in a row of shrubs, so bland-looking that it wasn't a surprise to me she wasn't getting any marriage offers from any of the boys. Her father had a nice house, but he had spent all his money on it, so they weren't in a good place to help her find a husband. She blew some kisses and was all like, "Thank you, my dear. Thank you, my love." Then she noticed that one of the uglier girls was staring. The carpenter's daughter was like, "You okay, girl?" in a twang, totally in the voice of that badass bitch from that one super famous TV show abroad. The girl in question wasn't responding, which is why the girl who was always tailing the carpenter's daughter pushed the wig off her eyes and was like, "Girl so mute she can't talk." She snapped her fingers in a circle and bobbled her head, and the carpenter's daughter put her hand on the friend's blouse. She was like, "Why, girly, being a little stiff in the water don't make no reason for a girl to be shy." I had no idea what she was saying, and none of the girls did either, but all of them turned from their mirrors and chuckled at the girl like she was the ugliest thing, and the poor girl shrunk tighter, holding in her tears and then making her exit from the house.

I was on my way out with the dirty plates, so I thought about pulling her by the shoulder and making some joke to make her feel good about herself, of course nowhere in the proximity of the carpenter's daughter, because I wasn't about to commit social suicide, but when I made my way out and was dropping the plates off by the bucket of water, someone was shaking the fence stronger than the wind, ramming it harder and with more intent than a goat. I saw the hump of a girl's rear and the ends of a bright orange dress and the trail of a ponytail swinging like a bell chime, and heard her calling her ex-best friend's name. It was obviously the milkmaid. I went back in and was like, "I don't know if you can hear it with all the clatter up in here, but your friend has come to see you." The carpenter's daughter peeked out for a second then dove back onto her cot, huddled next to her best girl friends, and whispered something to the group. She came up to me and was like, "Milker, can you answer her?"

I was like, "Why not?" People who knew me well knew that the reason why I was called Milker by everyone was because back in the day, I was one of the few people who felt like helping the milkmaid with her deliveries. That was some years back, and I knew more than anyone that if I ever left this village, the name Milker was going to be attached to something else I did, and with none of the irony of my village past. Even so, I didn't mind talking to her, and did so once in a while when I wasn't with the girls who were more like girls and able to understand me. I walked onto the patio, trudging through the dust in my slippers, and gave a little wink at that goat right beside her that just loved to stare. The milkmaid was so busy shouting the names of everyone in the carpenter's family that she didn't seem to notice me. I was like, "Girl, you have no volume control, and no shame, either." I put my arm into the hole in the fence and gave her a pat on the shoulder.

She was like, "Hey, Milker." Some of the girls who were staring from the door gasped, but I rolled my eyes. I was like, "Hey back. What's going on?" "Nothing good. How are your brothers?" "They're good." "How are your parents?" "Doing what they always do." Then, she was like, "Is that marriage proposal still on the table?" I snorted. I was using the 'I'm too young' card to not marry, and she was so quick in rejecting the offer that my father tore up my proposal picture and threw it in the fire. I was like, "Why do you ask?" She was like, "I have something to ask you later, but I need to talk to someone else first." I understood. I stared back towards the patio and was like, "Hey, girl, talk to your best friend." This queen, taller than the sun with her blonde wig on, her nails done, groaned at her girls loud enough for us to hear it here, but she eventually came outside, with a few of her girls gathered around her like a posse. The milkmaid was like, "I need to speak to you privately." The carpenter's daughter opened the door in the fence and was like, "Whatever you can say to me you can say in front of anyone else."

The milkmaid came up to the patio and did something weird. She kicked an imaginary ball back and forth with her feet, and then thrust her foot toward the host. She was like, "Remember when I told you I was going to be the first professional football player from here, and you … you talked about how you would be the first professional dancer from here, and we would talk ... we would talk about the days we would go to the city ... and live together ... perform together ... and we burned dolls pretending they were like the us ... the us that didn't belong here?"

The milkmaid looked like she was about to tear up. The girls who normally cackled freely at others sat on the patio and looked away. I was also getting a little teary, remembering the day when we were little kids in the field, and it was hot, and I was sticky, and I wanted to go inside, and all the boys were making fun of me for not being able to kick a ball straight, and the milkmaid took the ball from me and passed it to someone else, and a boy said maybe she and I should pray that our bodies and souls might switch places like in that old movie, and she straight-up decked him and broke some of his teeth, and we became friends.

The milkmaid was like, "What have you been telling everyone?" The carpenter's daughter was getting tired of standing, so she sat down on the patio, her arms around her waist. She was like, "What do you *think* I've been telling them?" The milkmaid was like, "I don't want to say it." The carpenter's daughter was like, "Well, if you are so quick to defend what you think is a lie, why can't you tell me what you think the lie is?" The carpenter's daughter wasn't talking straight. I decided to take the milkmaid aside to the other side of the carpenter's house. When we got there, I was like, "Hey, girl. The truth is this. A week ago, the carpenter's daughter gathered most of the girls, and of course an honorary member of the group like me, at her house. She made a big show of saying that she wanted to watch a movie that her brother brought her from the city, but really she just wanted to spread gossip. She made sure we were all comfortable on our cots, and we had a little heel-walking competition, and then she gathered us around her cot. She said she didn't want to be mean, and the last thing she wanted was to change our opinions of a dear friend, but she knew a secret, and it affected all of our lives. Apparently, her good friend told her she had lost her virginity to a man twice her age."

The milkmaid interrupted me with a "What?" It was a surprise for all of us, too. I had been licking the insides of my teeth thinking about the first time I did it, while most of the girls gasped since most of them couldn't dare imagine having so much as a hand on their breasts before marriage. I was like, "Yeah. She was a good actress, too. She held her friend's hands, gasped like she was going to faint, told them to give her their strength so she could press on and tell her tale. She started calling this friend of hers a demon, and said the friend had confessed about her first and fifth and eighth and ninth time doing it, and said she'd done it with different men, describing the positions and all of it. The carpenter's daughter claimed that she had told her to think of her body, and of her future husband. She said her friend just laughed, called her a baby, and said something about a disease she had that would make a grown-up gasp at its name."

The milkmaid was like, "What does that have to do with me?" I tapped her cheeks and sighed. I was like, "Because, one of the girls, who had atrociously long fingernails, so ugly, I swear, guessed, like anyone who knew anything about the girls in this village, that it was you." The milkmaid stepped back and was like, "What?" again. I was like, "Yeah. The carpenter's daughter gasped, fanned her hands and denied it, but the girl with the carrot nails said it had to be you, because every boy wanted to marry you, and it was obvious you had seduced them. The carpenter's daughter didn't deny it; she just sighed at the horror of it all and asked for us to pray." I was about to say more, but the milkmaid stormed back to where the carpenter's daughter was and kicked the fence. I caught up to her while she was like, "I come to you, afraid and alone, and you start telling people things?" The carpenter's daughter was like, "You're the one who told me what you told me. I've been telling people what they need to hear for their own safety." The milkmaid got in position to kick her friend. She was like, "That's a fucking lie." All the girls gasped at her for cursing. I thought she was going to knock some teeth in. Instead, she stood straight up and was like, "Why are you telling them these things? You know they're not true."

The carpenter's daughter stood again, took off the wig, revealing a pair of short, tidy braids. She was like, "Do I? I only did what was best for our community."

The milkmaid was like, "It's all a lie! Why are you telling them lies? I don't have a mother ... I don't have a father ... I need to get married ... but now, now ... there's nothing for me ... I..." She ran away so fast the dust flew.

The door in the fence had been left open. A few goats had wandered onto the property and were chewing the manicured grass. The carpenter's daughter turned back to her friends. The one with too much mascara on was like, "Slut." The big-belly friend was like, "Yeah, she's a real slut, for sure. We should have never let her in." The friend who had spent the whole time reading her magazine was like, "She's probably going to cough in our milk and give us her disease." The girl who had been made fun of earlier in the day and who never spoke said, "For sure." The girls looked at her, surprised she wasn't mute. She went on, "Such a dumbo." Dumbo was what my mother called the senile dog that kept getting lost in the rubber trees outside our house. The other girls liked that, and were like, "What a dumbo. What a dumbo, for sure." Everyone headed back in, but the carpenter's daughter stopped me at the patio and put her finger to my mouth. She was like, "I don't know if it's a good idea to keep letting a boy in here. You understand, don't you?"

It was awkward to look into her eyes, because I couldn't be all like, "Well, you both are my friends, so I can't let you walk all over her any more than if she was using you for a popularity spurt." Instead, I checked my messages, the only thing being those goat chirpings my mother had accidentally sent me. I put my phone up to my ear and pretended to listen to it, and was like, "Sorry dear, but I have other lunch plans. Tata, toodles, adieu." None of those goodbyes were in any language spoken around here, so she didn't understand any of them, but the girl was pointing me off the property anyways.

As I made my exit, I cursed the long walk ahead of me. The carpenter and his family had built their hut as far as possible from the main road, in part to hide the fact that they had the only house in the village that was made of wood. The closest thing to civilisation anywhere close to their house was that concrete hub of government apartments. I wasn't looking forward to being stared at by all of the female folk who could always be found outside it, cooking around fires, staring into random windows, and trading gossip. Beyond that was the field, where the boys always stopped kicking their ball around to chuckle at the swish of my steps, while the goatherd stared at me with two savage coals for eyes.

My stuttered swagger was taking me to the only place I knew I could be. Changing course a little, I ended up at the opening of his mud hut, and found him there, alone, waiting most likely for the grandmother with the potato snack basket to pass by so he could get something for his three-year-old son. I put my sandals outside and locked the door coming in. He was like, "You, what are you doing here?" but I wasn't going to let him talk; I had already taken my pants off. I pushed him back onto his cot and took off the wrapping around his legs and played with his thing with my lower side to his face. He was turning away and was like, "Don't do that." I was rubbing his front side against my back side and saying, "But you love it." He did something I had never seen him do before. He pushed me off and tied his wrapping back on. Not that it was helping; if anything, I was getting hornier, the way his thing was sticking out of it. He was like, "I was talking to the preacher about my afflictions a few days back. He said he was going to help me become a better man, which I think is what is best for me." I lay on my side with my pubes out for him to see, pretending to finger myself, and I was like, "But, there's nothing wrong with what we do. You like it, I like it, so we're happy." The man inside of him was chuckling, and he was like, "You know nothing about me. I'm not happy in the least."

I wrapped myself around his back and gave him a little peck on the cheek and held him by his thing while I was leaning into him. I was like, "I know what you feel, I swear," and the only thing he was able to say was something like, "Don't touch me." He meant it, too. The way he pushed me, almost bruising my hip bone as I slammed against the mud of his floor, I was afraid he was going to hit me. He had lost his erection and was standing over me, his fists clenched. I was zipping my pants back up while he was telling me something like, "Are you that much of a faggot? You're only sixteen, and I'm almost fifty. How do you think you can understand what it means to have a family? How do you think it's right for you to strip yourself in the bed where I sleep with my little boy? Get out of my house, now. I said, get out of my house now!" He was yelling at me with such a crazy voice he didn't have to tell me twice. I stumbled out of his hut and into the heat. I was already sweating so much on my neck just feeling the pounce of his words that the sun added nothing to my misery. I was planning all the things I was going to tell him. I was going to be all like, 'Just because I'm young doesn't mean I can't understand things,' or 'I've lived just as bad a life as you have; it wasn't like my father gave me love or much of anything,' or 'I'll be a father to your kid, I can be just as much as a wife as your real one. All you have to do is love me.' The worst part of it all was remembering that these were all things I was never going to be able to say to him, because he had really locked that door. I looked at that app and saw that he was no longer next to me, that he really was such a mature almost fifty-year-old that he was going to block me, and I could have screamed at those nosy goats who were looking up from munching on the wild grass to watch me leave. I could have made them so scared that they would think twice before they ever looked at a person again.

On the way back to my home,
the missus washing her copper basket outside
was giving me a bit of a mad eye.

(Milker)

I was used to the staring, but I stared back.
She put her hibiscus tea to her mouth and shrunk into her shawl.
There were more puffs on a dandelion than strands on her scalp,

and she spoke to this other friend of hers, softly.
Paltry, *wizened*, and *frail*.
Those were the words I would have used to describe her.

Just outside our hut,
the boys were coming home from their games,
slapping each other's asses and laughing out loud at me.

Remember that when one is
— how to say —
insecure, *curt*, and *self-conscious*, all at once,
it is easier to hide in the company of others.
A wolf in a pack appears more daunting than one,
especially when one is hunting a bear.

I didn't care anymore.
This was me at the end of the day,
whether he wanted to be a part of it or not.

There was a reason why philosophers preached
self-love over all else,
because if we accept our own body or mind,
no matter their condition,
on the day when the clock reverts to zero,
and our bodies become dust,
we will be at the right place.

I pretended to be one of those divas,
from the TV show I was meant to be in,

and let the dust lash my body,
like it was the cape I was meant to wear.

If the mind is a chalice, mine was full of expired wine, and in the outer rings of this cup, the words of this auntie rang again and again. "Just a year married, and it's all gone. What a shame." I supposed in the capital or in the hometown of our newest family guest — a stranger to us until a few months back, now a staple at all our family gatherings — men and women would certainly say such things about each other. But even they would never fathom doing so while they were sitting across the person in question. 'It had been six months since the Incident,' they would think to themselves. 'Why do these people have the gall to say such things every week?' My father would have called them *brazen*. I would have preferred *brutish*. If he were still alive, he could have asked me, 'Dearest, the aunties have been talking behind your back for many years. Considering the profession you chose, haven't you gotten used to it yet?' and I could have responded, 'I am used to them lambasting my writing, or calling me a whore behind my back, but never pitying me.' I also knew that I wasn't a whore, that my husband and I were very happily monogamous, and that anything I wrote about in my articles, I discovered only with him. It was easy to discard what anyone said when they were lying, but much harder on the heart when what they said had an element of truth.

When I tuned back in to the two aunties, relatives on my husband's side, they were changing the subject. I already knew about their habit of dominating the conversation at family events. One of them had held an entire audience hostage during our wedding reception as she held forth on the taste of figs, which she said varied depending on whether they were directly harvested or stored too long in the freezer or refrigerator. Now the two women were doing it again, directing traffic like a couple of wily old beat cops. The older woman pointed to my husband's distant cousin, who was sitting on the other side of a vase, and said, "If his mother had taken the time to teach him the language, he would be speaking well now." I had always assumed that this cousin, who was a world-wizened journalist, would have been accustomed to any and all cultures, but the auntie's words suggested otherwise. The woman who was talking to this auntie, the mother-in-law to the man the journalist was talking to, said equally loudly, "Remember that he has only been here for a little over a half-year. He is doing his best..." She could not say any more. Culture dictates that when speaking to an elder, there is a certain point up to which one could speak, and never with a tone of disregard. The auntie knew the value of her thinning greys had come, and she nodded accordingly while the other auntie's sentences trailed off. She talked loudly about some other youngster. I was distracted, as my husband's sister came to serve the relatives tea and small biscuits, along with cut bananas and wild berries.

My husband was normally quite sociable at these family gatherings, but tonight he was taciturn. He had told me earlier in the morning that he had something to show to the inheritor of Great-Auntie Lyrica's blood. The matter was urgent enough that he had retreated to the stucco of his sister's library and spent most of the afternoon there. *Reluctance* to concern himself with the needs of a stranger was how my father would have seen it, but I had known my husband since tenth grade; he was certainly into his books, but he was also the first person to speak up to a stranger. *Outgoing, affable, warm-blooded,* these were the words that many a stranger would have applied to him even after knowing him for a short time, but after the Incident, my body changed, and so did his mind. I concentrated on other things, but I had few options. The other family members were not in the living room but in other rooms, taking strolls to inspect the photos on the walls or attending to the needs and whims of their children. I had no desire to stay and listen to these two aunties. or to my husband's two cousins, who were having an equally blunt conversation. This cousin from outside the city had wanted to practise the language and was throwing around all of the phrases and small words he had learned during his short stay. Unfortunately, he happened to sit next to the family's least sociable relative, a young man infamous for sitting in a corner with his phone and playing mobile games during family gatherings. Oddly, the two men were now talking. They appeared to have struck up a sort of stunted, one-way friendship. The journalist said what he could, this cousin of ours responded with one-word answers, but otherwise kept his attention on his phone. A less introspective person would have trailed off the conversation into some general statements, but his eyes were flickering in thought, as mine would be. *Human nature, solitude, decadence* were some of the words he had shoehorned into his question, but the sentence was too incoherent to be understood, and the cousin just smiled weakly while keeping his face to the phone. Our journalist cousin kept trying to phrase the question over and over again, with no success. He never gave up practising.

Later, his wife came along with their daughter. They went to speak with his mother, knowing how much of a pain it was to have any sort of small talk with this man. His daughter carried a bowl with her goldfish in it to every social event she attended. *Endearing* was how I viewed it several years ago; *cumbersome* was how I saw it shortly after that. I still thought she was preferable to her brother, who greeted us all with his magic tricks. The goldfish bowl dripped water all over the hardwood floor, but these aunties listened intently to every word the girl said. I knew they would never do this for any girl over the age of sixteen, since that would involve talking about real things like periods or sex. I had to be grateful in a way, for if these selectively supportive aunties had ever talked to me openly about my own urges, I might never have taken up the pen. My father told me that even other women would dismiss me, but that with time, my words would find value, as time had done for my husband's auntie, as time would do for his own words. Sadly, my father's stories withered on the bookshelves for many decades before they went out of print. After the Incident took its own toll on my body, I wondered often if he let himself be consumed by chronic disease because he had long died on the inside. I would have wished for something similar, but my body was not afflicted by any such thing. The devil must have signed a contract with me while I was in that hospital bed, unconscious, that I would return to life, but on the condition that no other life would be able to spring from me.

"We have to go," my husband said, interrupting me as I was drinking a cup of chamomile tea. My palm shook as it had that day I fainted.

"Has something else happened?" I asked.

"No, nothing like that. We are going back home."

I looked at the mess I had made, all over the coaster, all over the table, etched out of the stained glass.

"You did not have to speak so seriously," I said as I got to my feet. "I thought we came here to see family, not to look at books."

My husband was not responding to me. He was talking to his cousin, the one who worked as a journalist in the capital.

"Are you coming?" he asked. As the journalist made his way to our car and offered to sit in the back seat, despite being offered the front, I asked myself the simple question, 'When did they have the chance to speak?' I had observed everyone in my vicinity for the last few hours, during lunch particularly, and there was not a single moment when these two crossed paths. I supposed that they had spoken enough here or there during the last few family gatherings that it was plausible they talked on the phone when I didn't notice, and I did go to the toilet fairly regularly, and my father warned me that no matter how much a writer's spirit leans towards clairvoyance, we will never truly be psychics or mystics, for we are humans who can err as easily as anyone else. It was not hard to reflect on the failings of humanity. I did not know much about the Incident, I was simply one of its victims who had fainted in her car while she was stuck in the suburbs driving. I did know that it was named the Incident, and that there had been protests, and that during one of them, the CEO of the pesticide plant responsible for the leakage had labeled the entire calamity 'a mere incident.' I also knew that while the poisoning never reached the verdant cottage where my husband's sister lived in the hills far from the lake, everything else along the drive from her cottage to our house had seen something of the Incident's effects. At the end of the hill and at the edge of the forest was once a vibrant neighborhood of wooden cottages. Each of them had a "For Sale" sign over their doors, for that many of the people of the neighborhood had passed on, and whoever was left most likely preferred to settle elsewhere. The road ringed towards the lake before returning into a crevasse under a hill. The skeletons of birds and bears littered the lawns. They were dying in waves, along with their prey. The water had been cleared of the rotting fish and mustard-coloured waves, but the smell of the chemical waste was still there, and even if the smell was fading, it was something we could never forget. The two cousins were immersed in conversation, but nothing escaped their eyes. One cousin was telling my husband that his reporting had grown to be such a success that his team had stationed him here to collect more personal stories, and to document what my cousin had termed, in the national language, "the rebirth."

"The people here..." he said, "they are warriors ... five hundred years ago ... they were warriors ... fifty years ago ... they were warriors. We survive this. We survive that. We live on."

My husband, who was much more fluent in our language, was so distracted by his own thoughts he almost ran over a crossing deer. The poor thing looked starved, ready to be hit by a car, as there were no longer things for it or its fawn to feed on, though the winter had ended.

"Yes, yes, yes!" my husband said. "We were the main nomads of the continent many centuries back, taking swathes of land as ours, left and right. Then, we lost all of it, one by one, to kingdoms to the east and west, but we never forgot who we are. The north may have had us in their pockets for the last half-century, but we won't stay there.

Once our standards of education return to how they were many centuries ago, once we get over the Incident and any other tragedy corruption and mismanagement throws our way, we will go back to doing great things, I am sure."

I was equally sure that only about eight percent of my husband's speech reached his cousin's comprehension, and had I been in the debating mood, as both of us had often been during our courtship, I would have voiced that opinion. I imagined goading him with statistics on language and the nation. 'Excluding the two of us,' I might have said, 'look at how many people under the age of thirty are more fluent in the national language than they are in their mother tongue. Look at how much they stare at their mobile screens, and at the voting tendencies of the last twenty years, and you will see that everything you dare to predict is very much heading in the opposite direction.' Though I said not a single word of this, my husband's cousin stared at the back seat, seemingly aware of my scepticism. *Telepathy.*

"You also write," he said.

"What he means to say is that I had told him previously that you write for a local magazine," said my husband, in an attempt to clarify.

"What my husband means to say," I clarified in return, "is that I write for one of the gossip magazines, something a little *smutty*, something a little *coquettish*, nothing that he would believe that a journalist as *esteemed* as yourself should learn about, and so he has wrapped me up in a simple bow, saying I am nothing but a writer for a local magazine."

My husband chuckled and opened his window again. His cousin wanted to say something he would be unable to express unless he switched languages.

"I have actually read some of your articles," he said. "In translation, I mean, and in one of the liberal-leaning newspapers. They were very instructional..." *Too coy*, he was, to say in which sense. "But I haven't seen your writing in many months."

"I no longer have anything to write about," I said. The car was silent then.

"Well, if you have any clippings of anything you are working on, I would love to read them," said the journalist in this cousin of ours. "I'm not so good at reading yet, but if I work at it with my dictionary, I am sure I could give you feedback."

"I doubt what she writes is anything you want to use to practise our language," quipped my husband. Too florid language for a sex column, he would say, long before he was afraid such criticisms would lead to a lack of sex.

"To think, this was once coming from my biggest fan," I quipped back. "What he and I did in private was what I later coined as the 'umbrella position.' Well, 'missionary position,' or 'pretzel position,' or 'umbrella position,' the only one my husband has learnt of late is how to sleep well in the guest bed."

The silence for the rest of the car ride was more than guaranteed after having said that. My husband and his cousin eyed the thistles of the pine trees, the slopes of the drive melting into daffodils and tulip blooms. No one spoke, and when we finally reached our home, another one of the many indistinguishable cottages, one-storey, and of wooden walls, the stained-glass windows, purple and red and pink, my husband got out without opening the door for me or waiting for me to follow. My father had warned me that all relations between loved ones grow ugly with time, after people are used to one another and grow tired of faking affection, but I noticed that my husband had no courtesy for his cousin either. He ran to the front door, opened up everything, and as his cousin and I reached the house, he made a point to inform us that he had a leaflet of great importance that he needed to show to his guest. He hid himself upstairs, this time in his own personal library.

"He says ... mother's house ... he must be showing," his cousin said.

"I don't understand," I responded back. He tried to piece together another, more discernable sentence, but I led him to the sofa, gestured for him to sit down, and went to the kitchen to prepare him tea. I could not help but steal a glance at myself in the mirror. I had put on one of the brighter lipsticks that had not yet expired, as well as mascara, and before all that I had used a good-quality skin cleanser and moisturiser, and yet my eyes looked fatigued. I glanced at the living room to notice the cousin had stood up and was staring at the books above the TV. He was looking at my husband's books, *An Introduction to Modern Literature*, *History as Myth*, *The Repercussions of Faith*, and then the booklets my husband had made of our family's genealogy, which sat on the second shelf. The tea whistled, and I brought it to his side.

"No need, I am not thirsty," he said, and, as is custom in this region, he rejected the offer with both of his hands on his chest.

"I insist," I said, and I went to a hidden cabinet on the other side of the bookcase to retrieve cookies. "And you must eat these as well. They are of a gooseberry flavour you will never find in your hometown."

When I had offered, he had only taken one, but after taking a taste of the mild bitter and yet gushing paste, he asked for many more. We sat waiting for my husband for what seemed like a long time. This cousin of his and I had nothing much to say. I looked outside our house, staring at the garden we started, where the begonias were famished, the grass was decrepit, and the bare trees made their consternated faces at the weeds. The clouds were puffing and paunching, symptoms of a swift but heavy rain to pass in the coming hours. I thought of the buildings far in the distance, a block of black cubes of ten storeys each. *Modern* or *postmodern*, this is what my father would have called the design, or he would have mumbled more specific words as he read his books or sketched. He would have been more successful if he had worked harder on his own ideas or found himself lost in the beauty of his work rather than fussing about the styles of others long deceased. He would have had much to complain about in the way my husband had decorated our house. Our tables were covered in vases or charms made by my husband's father, his divans had ornamental pillows and sheets knitted by his mother. I did not like to look at such *gauche* things, but my father had told me that everything created by a human was a moment of history, and that one line had instructed me that every possession had something in it to be appreciated. I had heard this cousin speak up, but I hadn't heard him, so I pricked my eyebrows, gave the full attention of my two eyes to the man with the long jawline, the lucid green eyes, and my husband's brown skin. He had switched languages once more, to be a hundred percent clear.

"My cousin told me about you. I'm sorry for what you have been through."

I picked up a magazine from under the table and folded it.

"At least I am not dead," I said.

"I know," he said. "I've heard many stories for the article, but I don't think any of them were nearly as devastating as what happened to you. Do you mind talking about it?"

Words are like pain. The moment we notice pain's presence is the same moment we dwell on it and allow it to irritate us to the point nothing else can exist.

"My story is stupid," I said, but he disagreed.

"I've interviewed a man who claimed his greatest feat was raising a potato shaped like a man. That was a stupid story."

I respected his smile. Since he was a man who rarely gave one, I had the impression that when he smiled, it came from the tip of his corneas and nowhere near his mouth. It was accordingly genuine.

"What is your question?" I asked him.

"I heard a handful of stories here or there about women whose children died in their arms as they were walking. I remembered how they described the way their bodies would cough uncontrollably and cramp in all the wrong places. There were women who had been pregnant and miscarried as a result of the gas, and women whose reproductive organs were damaged to the point they would never become mothers. I heard of them when I spoke to the doctors at the hospitals, but I never met one. So, I wanted to ask you, how does it feel to be told you can never bear children?"

I suddenly felt like I was in that hospital bed again, losing my senses of sight and smell.

"Well, my husband told me he loved me no matter what happens."

'What a stupid answer,' he should have said. 'Is all that matters to you, what your husband thinks? What about your own dreams? Tell me the truth. How does it feel, for every auntie or neighbour to shake their head and call what happened a shame behind your back, but never ask you how you are doing? How does it feel, to know you're never going to have the one thing you built a marriage on? How does it feel, to be barren?'

"I met my husband when I was fairly young and a lot less sure of myself than I am now. I always had this *enormous* respect for him, because since he was half the age he is now, he knew two things, that he loved history, and that he wanted nothing more than to be a father. I had long renounced my own father's religion, and I was more into getting stoned than any girl of that generation would care to admit, but I agreed on that other one thing, that I loved the idea of motherhood. Certain things about me changed. Over time, I became more willing to speak my mind, more comfortable with my body, a lover of exploration and adventure, but I still wanted children. We were going to be prepared. To be writers in a country like this meant that for both of us money was scarce. We were going to plan correctly, save up the proper amount, and give them the life our parents could never afford for us. The truth was what he had told me, a week after the Incident, when the gynaecologist told us in the hospital what had happened to me, when he had said that children were a responsibility that he still wasn't ready for."

It was a shame that he had to reach this conclusion in the middle of research and not after a set number of findings.

"My husband and I might seem distant now, but it was nothing like that. The first night of our marriage, I couldn't fall asleep, because I had never been with a man before, and just the idea of making love to someone I cared for so much, but with a body much more rounded than it appeared to be while clothed, made it hard for me to remove my undergarments. So, my husband set me down on the bed, put my head and its thumping thoughts next to his beating chest, and he sang me a lullaby. It was what his own mother sang when he was a little child. The lullaby reminded me that the beats between his heart and my head were what connected us, and I was later able to love. Every time I think of that song, I remember that it was a song passed through generations of mothers, sung to him because one day it would be taught to me, so that I could sing it to our own child. It made me comfortable to mount him, to kiss him passionately, and afterwards, almost every day, we did these intimate things, and I learned everything about myself, and I felt angry at the world for teaching me to condemn acts that should have been worshipped. It is why I picked up where my father left off and got fame in a small town for being willing to speak my mind. Believe me, we have tried to get back to how it used to be, but a lot has changed for us this year, and it just isn't working..."

So said this broken hourglass, spilling sand over the edge, flooding my thoughts to the point that each kernel dropped through my nerves, trickled into my chest, and stained my heart one inch closer towards being cracked. I had to look up at our hideously beige ceiling to prevent myself from crying.

"Don't let what I say mislead you. I love my husband, almost too much. When I was younger, people asked me when I realised I was in love with the man I would marry, and I would refer to those petty childish moments before our marriage, like when he first took me out to dinner on a teenager's budget or how he proposed to me in the rain. Now, if any other person were to ask me when I fell in love with him, I would answer that it could have been in any of the moments when he relieved me of my anxiety with a touch of his hand. I don't think love can be based on a key moment anymore. It's based on a lifetime of support and setbacks, and if there's one man I trust to be there more for me, it's going to be him. I just wish I could be there for him."

I had more to say, but my husband was coming downstairs, making the stairs creak loudly, with a book full of notes. He threw them onto his cousin's lap, opened the pages and pointed with a highlighter.

"Did you know that your great-grandfather owned a private mansion on the edge of the lake?" my husband said in our language. From the way his cousin nodded in mid-sentence, he had not understood. My husband switched languages. "You see ... your mother, Lyrica ... our great poetess ... yes, yes, very great writer. Look at the map. Here, not there. That! That place is where she wrote ... her best poems, super! I thought the property was sold, but it wasn't ... it should still be in her name!"

So *exuberantly* were the words coming from one side of my husband's mouth to our ears that he switched languages, spoke about other things, and neither of us could follow him. He wrote some things on a piece of paper in a mix of both languages and put it into the pocket of his cousin's blazer. He looked at the two of us and noticed that our eyes were not able to meet his.

"I'm sorry," he said. "Was I interrupting something?"

I picked up his tea and put it on a tray that I was on the way to wash in the kitchen.

"It's nothing," I said. "He was asking me some questions, doing research, I believe, for one of the articles he will write for the newspaper."

It was guaranteed that my husband was going to gripe after his cousin had left that he had expressly forbidden me from speaking about my personal history. I turned with the tray in my hands back in their direction, but due to nothing my husband had said.

"That isn't true at all," his cousin said in his language. "Everything you said was off the record. You are family. I only wanted to get to know you better."

"That is how someone from here would think," said my husband in our language, and he wrapped his arm around his cousin in a way he almost never did with other men. I couldn't stand the sight of them for much longer. I had to sigh out these tears, and from under their droplets was returned something that he had given to me earlier, not a smile, but a beam, erring on the side of the genuine.

(The Sex Columnist)

I served my husband and his cousin another round of tea, finding that I was quite comfortable with them both.
I came to my husband's side,
and for the first time in a while,
I massaged his shoulders gently.

It was like touching sapphire, or silk.

My husband asked if his cousin needed help finding the house.

He said it was something he wanted to do by himself,
and when I agreed, my husband rubbed his hand against my
knee.

I couldn't help liking the way it felt.

I couldn't help releasing my breath,
imagining that perhaps once our cousin left, ·
I could have a chance to pounce on his chest,
and freckle my husband with kisses.

Now, the question was, whose necklace was it?
The area around my cart was a mess: napkins and plastic
bags to the left, the remains of someone's hamburger
splattered all over the right. Luckily, I had good eyes for
scouring from all those years handling peanuts and almonds
and spicing them with just the right amount of pepper or
cinnamon or salt, so it was easy to see what was glimmering
and shining on the cobblestone. It would have been nice if
that business lady in the grey suit with her hair in a bun had
been paying more attention to her phone or her peanut
order when I scooped it up. Same thing I thought seeing all
those boys with holes in their pants drawing something with
sticks in the trash. If they were the sons of who I thought
they were, that homeless woman who lived on the alley a
block or two off the Great Founder's Plaza, they could have
also been fishing for fancy things. Eleven o'clock to two
o'clock wasn't the time to be thinking about anything other
than the price of salted peanuts versus caramelised ones in

(The Peanut Vendor)

the first place. I sat back in the corner where my cart was, pushed my feet against the iron wheels and leaned back in my chair, all the while discreetly maneuvering the find of the day into my pocket.

Good thing there was a lot of other hubbub. The Great Founder's Plaza was nicknamed the Great Founder's Traffic Trap. It sat between a major bus station and the market, where all the tourists went to watch the slum people hawk their junk as "traditional." Whether it was two a.m. or two p.m, the plaza was always jammed with people. Today it was worse because of a gay parade on the other side of the main avenue. It wasn't anywhere close to here, but you could see the tourists in their rainbow wigs and dressed in drag taking photos of each other, and the locals, who weren't into any of these things, were crowding around to gawk and make comments. One of the locals was standing in line for my cart, waiting to buy a snack. It was really more of an attempt at a line, because no one in these parts — students, business folk, anyone who wanted a snack before or after lunch — had the patience to spend their one-to-two-hour break standing in the smog.

The couple in front of me looked like they had both won Mr. and Mrs. World titles. Arms like tree trunks, the latest athletic gear. I knew if my wife was here, she would have asked me to buy something like what the girl was wearing, a flaming silver jacket and denim sweatpants. The electricity was only on for half the day, and we didn't have enough water to do our laundry more than once a week, but she still thought she should have a new purse or a fleece coat. The guy and girl in front of me dressed like daily shoppers at Galaxy Mall, but at the moment they had other things on their mind besides clothes. After the girl asked for some peanuts, plain, no salt, and the guy asked for caramel and cinnamon on his, he put his hand on her bicep and asked, "So how do you get these?"

The guy was fondling her arm more than touching it. The girl started zipping her jacket up as an excuse to get him off of her, then pulled out her phone. She was looking at it when she said, "I'm usually busy at the gym, the one right outside of the Faculty of Sciences."

"No way! I'm always running at the gym, too. You know, the one right next to school. It's by the faculties of math and sciences, you know, the one with—"

He was putting his hands in and out of his pockets and squinting upwards, a fib in his eyes. If the girl ever took her eyes off her screen, she could have seen it herself. I finished roasting her peanuts and gave them to her. I was starting to work on the guy's order when I heard her ask him, "Why do you think we're here?"

"You don't like peanuts, baby girl? We can get whatever else you want. Ice cream, fried snacks, you name, it's all on me!"

"No, no. I mean, think about it. There are billions of stars in the sky, like there are billions of us. We populate, we build great empires, the empires fall, the populations die out, but we start over, all in the vain belief we're working towards something greater. Well, what if there isn't really something greater? What if this is what we really are, like ants? How can we believe we are meant to reach the stars?"

I was roasting his peanuts and thinking this was an odd time for a uni lecture about the universe, but the guy was just trying to keep up with his date.

"I never thought about that. It's nice to be around someone who makes me think a lot."

"What are you trying to do?" she asked. "Your lips are getting too close to my face."

I interrupted to ask, "Do you want a napkin?" because the oil was dripping out of the paper cone and was about to drip onto her clothes. Man to man, I was feeling sorry for the boy and at the same time feeling like he was lucky, because at least this girl was being direct with what she did or didn't want, unlike my wife. They were talking about something else in line, but I had to tell them to scoot, and they went off in separate directions, which was no surprise to me. I didn't have time to look at them anymore. I had my next customer to deal with. He was one of my regulars, a pencil pusher who worked in one of those small government buildings on the eastern side of the plaza. I always noticed his moustache. It was distinguished, like it belonged on a king. He ordered the special and asked, "You see the game last night?"

"Of course," I said, and recited the scores I had read in the paper. While I was scooping up his roasted peanuts, peppering them with cinnamon and letting them glaze in the honey, he jeered the name of the winning team and showed the number one with his finger. It was weird watching this suit-wearing bureaucrat, who was probably in his sixties, showing off his team spirit like he was in school. When I said nothing, he just stood there with his newspaper under one arm, sugar clumping all around his moustache like brine.

"You're quieter than normal," he finally said. My hand wasn't in my pocket, but I felt what was inside of it shake against my leg.

"Not really. I've always been a solitary kind of guy."

"No, no, no," he said, shaking his head so vigorously that the moustache sugar spread to his cheek. "What's wrong?"

In times like this, I would usually tell an outlandish story of something that actually happened, which was good for getting people to react. It wasn't a surprise to me, for example, that my wife and I fought yesterday, in that tarp held up by sticks we call a house, next to that bedsheet we cuddle under when it's warm enough to take it off the wall. I was looking through her phone and saw a lot of calls to people with male names, so of course I threw her phone at her while she was sitting on her stool, reading her gossip magazines, and called her a whore. She didn't even flinch. She turned a page of her magazine and said it was wrong for me to go through her phone, and my brother yelled from his side of the tarp that she was right. I told him it was none of his business, and he said just like it was none of my business to look through her phone. All of this from the guy who was supposed to be my flesh and blood.

"That's horrible," said the moustache guy. I didn't tell him the part where I listed all the names she had called, and my brother butted in to say a lot of those guys sounded rich and it wasn't a bad idea to get closer to them, or the part where I cursed my wife out and she told me she wouldn't speak to me if I talked like a street vendor, and I told her if she didn't like how a street vendor acted, she should have never married one, and she told me she wouldn't have married one if her father had given her a choice, and I ended up tearing that blanket from the wall into feathery fluff.

"Real awful stuff," I said. The man gave me some extra money, and I gave the man some extra peanuts. "So, what always brings you to these parts? You look like you belong downtown with that stopwatch and tie."

"Why, thank you," he said. I wasn't saying it as a compliment, but he liked the opportunity to show off the gadgets on his wrist. "I work in the stock exchange building a little up the avenue."

"Must pay well."

"Not too much, no, and our money gets eaten up by the rent. We live a few blocks up from Galaxy Mall. But, hey, you do what you got to do because you love it, right?"

Or, he said something like that. I was too busy serving the three or four other guys ordering peanuts while he was talking.

"Yeah," I said, "that area around Galaxy Mall is nice, but expensive."

"Yeah, yeah," he said, and he went on and on about living expenses. "Where do you live?"

"Just on the street on the other side of the clock tower."

"Oh."

Ding-ding-ding! His eyes drew wide with the realisation that, believe it or not, people who worked as street vendors probably did not always come from the safe parts of town. It was dawning on him that he could be talking to someone who might live in a tent or a box with tin drum walls — a miscreant, a vagabond, whatever else the nighttime news called the people who lived where we did. He was sweating like it was two in the afternoon in the middle of summer. He fumbled for a response and failed. He was lucky the next guy in line was another regular, a guy who came around drunk and kept ordering popcorn and fried chicken and other things I didn't sell. Mr. Moustache said something about paperwork, and I'm pretty sure he left thinking I was waving him off, when really I was trying to flap the drunk's hand off me.

The drunk finally left, rush hour sorted itself out, and the sun retreated into a pocket of clouds. This gave me a little time to rest. I was just hanging around, spacing out, when I came across the last person I wanted to see: a one-armed lady who hung around the plaza. She had made a little space for herself on the steps leading to the Great Founder's statue. She lay on the bronzed step with her empty side — the side with the missing arm — facing up. No one was going to touch her or ask her to move. They would be too scared. I heard rumours from the boy who ran the meat pie stall that she was a terror at night, beating up men who were doing things with the prostitutes or taking girls away from the tin drums they called homes. I never saw that side of her because she usually slept during the day, giving me a full view of all the pus and flakes she called skin, her hair matted enough to house a family of birds, and her strange, oversized clothes, which doubled as her bedding. She had taken off her skirt and was using it as a blanket, and her jacket was wrapped around her breasts. Maybe it was because I happened to be looking at her, but she stirred awake, and in a peculiar way. She gasped loudly and rolled her body into a ball, as if she were being jumped. Then her eyes opened and she looked at everyone, one by one, the way the heavens are supposed to judge the guilty. This was all routine, but suddenly her eyes bulged open as though a bell had gone off in her head. She stood up, patted the pocket of her jacket and clutched it like it was a part of her heart. Then she stared at me so intently and for so long that I finally had to look away.

I turned away and checked in my pocket for the necklace, then took it out to inspect it more closely. It was chipped, not really gold but some fake, coated metal, and it had three bulbs for its design, with the middle one being the widest and the smaller two being encircled by diamond shapes. I felt a shadow trace over me. I hid the necklace under my shirt, and it fell to the ground. I looked to my left and right and even up and down, but no one was looking at me. I started thinking of my wife, and how good the necklace would look on her. She'd be so grateful that she'd wrap it around her hand, sit on my lap and pull down her hair, look into my eyes as the light of the orange fire played over her face, and then she would kiss me all over in a way she'd never done before.

Just as another customer left and I was picking up the necklace, I heard a woman's voice. "It's a beautiful necklace, indeed." I jumped up and knew right away that I was standing in the towering shadow of the one-armed homeless lady. My heart was racing but I tried to steady myself.

"Do you want peanuts or something?"

"No. I was only curious where you received such a fine-quality necklace," she said.

"That's none of your business," I said, and scooped some peanuts into a bag. "Sugar or caramel?"

"I told you I didn't want peanuts. Answer my question."

"Why do you care?"

"Because I saw you take it from a woman," she said, and nothing else. I was glad to live in a big city at times like this, because even though a lot of the other people in line heard, none of them cared. People around here follow street wisdom, which holds that no matter how interesting a conversation seems, if a person looks crazy, it's best to ignore them.

"It's a gift I got for my wife."

The lady banged her elbow onto my cart.

"Don't lie. It isn't the first time I've seen a pig flare up his little snout nose and discard his sins with a huff, and it won't be the last."

I smirked. Since I was a child people have commented on that fig-like nose of mine, and it was true I sighed a lot when people were trying to dig something out of me.

"Fine, but I didn't steal it from no one. I found it on the street, and as they say, finders keepers, losers weepers."

She huffed and pushed my cart so hard that it dumped salt and sugar all over my pants.

"Give me the necklace," she said, shoving her open palm under my face. Her skin was mottled and her forearm was covered in specks of dirt. "It belongs to one of the girls who lives on these streets. She needs it."

"What girl? There's no girl. I found it."

"Yes, and before you found it, it belonged to someone else. Give it back."

"I don't believe you for a second."

"You don't want to believe me, but the girl exists, and she needs that necklace more than you can imagine. Her parents left her with nothing. They used her as another set of hands to sell trinkets, or someone they could give to the landlord once in a while if they were short on cash. The heavens were kind, and her parents are long dead, but that necklace is one of the few things she earned that she never forked over to them. It's one of the few things which truly belong to her."

"Look, lady," I said. "That's a sad story and all, and I feel for people like that, and I would feel for them more, but my life isn't any better, and I need a necklace like this…" I was ready to tell her how important this necklace was to me —

how I was married to a woman I loved so much, but who every time I kissed her and called her beautiful would chuckle or remind me that our marriage was a joke. I didn't care that we were married because our fathers were best friends, or that I was convinced she and my brother were doing things when I was at work. "This is going to be the necklace which makes my wife fall in love with me."

No matter how good that one-armed woman was at looking serious, she was bad at hiding her laugh. The laugh was out of character, too, something you'd expect from those rich people out of cartoons who wear monocles and frilly clothes.

"Do you really think a plastic necklace is going to change how she feels about you?"

Oh, I was ready for that question. I was ready to tell her "no," end that sentence with a "but," and give some excuse that would make it all okay.

But, even in my imagination, that sentence never came. In a normal relationship, two people fall in love, ride the crest of their emotions until they marry, and then fall apart when they realise that the thrill is over. What could I possibly do to make my wife love me when we didn't even have that?

The one-armed lady looked south towards the buses.

"I have another appointment to attend. My Looker is calling me."

She clutched the dented space in her jacket, making it obvious that there was something much more dangerous under the cloth.

"Give me the necklace now."

I pulled out my pants pockets and showed her the inside of my shirt. Nothing. I gave her a little wink and said,

"Wherever the necklace went, it belongs to the fleas now." The one-armed lady groaned and said, "My bus is coming. When there are enough termites in the pantry to eat up the laces, I would rather exterminate the queen. We will play these games later. Ta-ta."

She crossed the plaza and got onto bus 86. Where she got the money for the fare I wasn't sure, but the 86 is the only one that heads in the direction of Galaxy Mall and the fancy hotel chains around it. I didn't sell many peanuts in the hour after she left. It was getting to be four, a time when most people had left the plaza unless they were tourists or really late for a bus. I mostly spent time with the necklace. I played with it around my hand, and I wore it for a bit on my own neck, but after hearing the one-armed lady's sob story, each time I felt it on me, it burned my skin.

There was a jacaranda tree growing out of the cobblestones between this cart and the popcorn vendor's. I thought if my wife or whoever lost it wasn't going to have it, the best place to put it was on one of its branches. It gave the bark a nice goldish hue. Whoever was meant to be the real owner of the cursed chain would find it there, and the whole thing would be out of my hands.

Their Decadence

I peeked in every crammed corner of my store, from the bags of chips hanging from the ceiling all the way to the wrenches and the scissors on the back side of the wall, and saw that it was empty of both customers and employees. The drinks hadn't been stolen. They were in a locked fridge. And the more valuable items weren't gone either. I would have heard clinking noises if they were taken. But the snacks on the racks were hard to count, which made them easy pickings. Where was my son? 'I'm busy doing schoolwork,' I imagined him saying. It had been a hot day, so I could understand why he preferred to stay in the comfort of our room and get his coursework done, but I had asked him to watch the store for me while I came from the city with more stock. I told the boys by the truck to unload everything, and by the time they finished giving me their boxes of potato chips and notebooks and sodas, I had bent under the counter and looked outside once. The main road was packed as usual, and it didn't help having a huge van blocking most of the road. I imagined the older man pulling his cart like a bull, saying, 'What are these strange cars doing here? Aren't motorcycles a hazard enough?' and I imagined the lady with the giant pail of water on her head crossing from the side of the trail to the side of the shacks on the other side of this row of stores and wondering, 'How much could I pay them to bring a month's worth of water to my home?' I didn't have to imagine the titters of the little boys and girls who didn't help at their mommy and daddy's stores, but who were allowed to play with the donkeys and goats instead. They were smirking at the sight of me. They at least had the excuse of being around nine, whereas my boy was nineteen. Where was he? I didn't have any time to sneak into the other side of the store, where we lived.

I did all the paperwork, paid off the van drivers, and had a chance to peek on the other side of the door by the counter, politely whispering my son's name. There were fruit peels all over the floor, and his clothes and books were scattered randomly around the racks. I found him sitting in the chair, right under the fan, playing with his phone, his legs crossed and his bare, muddy foot pointed into the air for anyone to see. I was going to shove him out of our house. I was going to do something much worse than yell. 'Is this all you do with your life?' I'd say as I threw him out. 'But, but, but—' he'd stutter, and I'd reply, 'No buts. Just get back to your post.' Which reminded me, no one was watching the store. I could hear my next customer already. 'Where have you been?' he'd ask, arms crossed, his bag of chips and cigarettes on the counter. 'I was... I was...' I'd say, trying to get back to the cash register, always so bad with excuses. 'Well, it's too late!' he'd say, and he'd slam the cigarettes onto the floor and leave.

No, people never cared as long as they got what they were looking for. They'd have probably gone, and I'd have no customers for the entire day, and it'd all be his fault. Oh, I should have yelled at my son. I was getting late.

"Excuse me ... son..."

He didn't look up from his phone. How many sons had the nerve to do that while a parent spoke to them, to sit there on the only chair in the room, a chair that was older than the boy himself, with his footprint on the only table in the house, a gift from the best carpenter in town, looking at his phone, with no other thoughts in his mind?

"Well ... I was thinking ... you know, it's not often your father gets called in like this ... and remember how you were supposed to look after the store ... you know..."

"Weren't you supposed to get the television fixed?"

I couldn't believe he could act this spoiled. My son was charming and independent, pursuing a good education at the cheapest college in the nearest city he could find. His phone bill may have been high, and I received a lot of messages concerning his grades, but whenever he came home on the weekend, he was polite and responsive, quick to come to the aid of his grandmother and assist in chores, always the sweetest, always on the first day, up to the twenty-third hour and fifty-ninth minute. The moment it turned midnight, he started sitting by the television, complaining about how there was nothing to do and asking for money. I got so used to it I actually had it set up as a reminder on my watch, and the only night he didn't do it was last night, because the television broke. I had told him a hundred times not to use it like a table, but since I was getting tired of his condescending reply, that he found it hard to manage with the lack of a table in what I called a common room, I stupidly let him put milk on top of the television, and since he is always doing multiple things at once, he knocked it down. He demanded the entire night that I get it fixed as soon as possible. I did call the repairman early this morning, and I assured him that it was to be fixed within the week. Now he was fiddling with the remote like it was the paw of a beloved pet that had died.

"It will be fixed soon..."

"Soon? You call a week soon? I'm leaving for the city soon, you know. I have exams to study for. Do you think I'll have time to watch television then? By the way, I never saw you call the repairman."

'Remember, you had a job to do,' I should've said, and kicked him out of the room, made him do some work.

"Let me call him again..." was what I said instead. He laid his head on the cushion and rolled his eyes.

'How dare you act so ungrateful,' I'd have said, and he'd roll his eyes, and I'd slap him. He'd touch his cheek, aghast that I, his father, of all people, could act angrily, and finally he'd remember that he was my son and that I was not his butler. He'd apologise, say something like, 'I'm sorry, Daddy dearest,' but I'd know he'd say it once and then go on to act the same way. 'Get out of the house!' I'd yell, and I wouldn't let him back in, no matter how many times he offered to help me at the store. Ooh, it was getting to that time where the sun was no longer beating you even inside of the house. There had to be people walking along the main road back to their shacks, looking for a store where they could buy some eggs or napkins or glue, noticing no one was around mine, and leaving for the next one.

"He's not picking up," I said. I waved the phone in his face as the 'line is busy' message played out.

"You don't have to show me you've done the bare minimum."

I was angry enough to throw that phone at his face, but I didn't have time. I needed to get back to work.

It turned out I didn't have any customers. Plenty of people were walking down the main road, but no one was looking at the plastic bags of cassava chips or puffed corn hanging from the ceiling, the chocolate powder or tea bags on the shelf. A kid was playing with one of the chickens cooping under the stairs, but he got chased away by one of the roosters. I went back behind the counter and stared out. Goats and sheep and wild dogs walked by, an older woman tried not to get swept up by the crowd or step on the dung of said animals. A woman passed her, eyes brown and bright like honeycomb, carrying her own weight in logs against her back. A boy almost tripped her as he skipped around. It was the summer holidays, so I didn't understand why he was wearing a school uniform. Another man was tugging a cart of bananas up the road. He was dressed like all of the other older men, who covered their legs with white wrap but never wore underwear, as the bulges and bulbs of their lower halves made all too clear. I should have started a charity to give them pants.

"Hello," said someone entering. It was one of my older customers, a guy whose wrap was always slipping a bit and showing too much of his thigh, along with the occasional flash of his groin. I went to shake his hand, and he took it, but with his left. He always held his wrap with his right, trying to make an ineptitude at tying into some cool pose.

"And, what are you looking for today, my friend?"

"I'll have my pack of cigarettes, please."

"Luckyies it is," I said, and I took them off the wall behind me.

As he paid, he asked, "Where were you earlier? I came and no one was around."

My hands clenched like they were crushing the fingers of my son. I told him I was dealing with family issues, and he chuckled and left. I opened the door, peeped into the common room. My son was still on that chair, tapping his phone. Ooh! 'Come over here and help with the store,' I was going to say. 'I'm busy,' he'd say, like always. I'd drag him by the ear, lock the door, and force him to sit at the stool and talk to whomever was on the other side of the counter while I'd go out and see if the hens had laid more eggs. 'Stay here until I say so,' I'd say, and he'd whine, or complain, but do what all good sons ought to do and behave. No, I was too mad to talk to him. I also had something else to deal with. There was the sound of the motorbikes and shuttle vans honking, and all of the people on the road were grumbling to each other and running towards something. Even this guy with the wrap got concerned enough to rush out of the store, keeping his arms wrapped around the waist of his wrap like a kid in need of the toilet.

"You have to come see this," he shouted at me from the outside of my store. I'd have never thought it, but for the first time in this middle-of-nowhere village, something strange was happening. It involved our milkmaid, who I recognised on the ground immediately because of the bright silk of her mother's orange dress. I'd watched her mother wear it when she was the one delivering milk, and I'd watched her wear it, too. The dimples on her lunar face were craters from this far out. All I could see on them was something of pain. It looked like a motorcycle accident, because she usually drove from her father's cow estate through the main road, parked her bike somewhere here, and walked among the huts all day. No, her motorcycle was still parked, but she had collapsed in the middle of the road, with all the conductors of the shuttle vans sticking their heads out to yell at her. Another thing, I could hear her yelping from here, saying something like 'I'm cured,' 'I'm lured,' or 'I'm pure,' along with obscenities and random sounds that made the shepherds with their trail of goats and calves pause in their walk. Everyone was stopping what they were doing to watch her, put their hands all over her, and say their prayers, but no one was helping her up.

I was going to go up to her and shout, 'Wake up, wake up.' I'd give her some water, carry her up to my store, call up the doctor in town, and wait with her for the thirty minutes it would take him to reach us by motorbike. She'd say, 'Thank you dear sir, I was just in the most horrible accident, but no one came to my aid,' and I'd say 'My dear, such is the moral decline of our village,' and she'd titter away. I didn't have time to imagine any more, because I really did leave my store to help.

"Wake up! Wake up!"

A few slaps to the face were enough to make her stir. She was conscious, but something had knocked the colour out of her flesh. The scene stirred the attention of others, albeit in the worst of ways. A man who was hauling cassavas in his cart stopped to stare. Some of the other men were coming out of their stores, but when they saw that a girl had fainted, they didn't act. The woman with the pail of water may have finally reached the other side of the road, but the commotion made her turn herself all the way back in this direction. She threw some of her water over the milkmaid, which made the girl come to her senses, and as she awoke, she pushed up her body, but dared not open her eyes.

"Stop it, stop it, stop it," she said. "I know my arms are blotchy, and there must be pus and pimples all over my face, but please, don't look at my body! It's not what you think! Believe me, please."

I didn't see anything like that at all. There was acne here and there, and she was developing an allergic rash over her chest, but her body, too curvy for a man of my age to feel innocent inspecting, was normal in pretty much every other way. I tried to lift her up, but I had trouble lifting some of the boxes. It was no surprise she was too heavy, and I fell over and almost broke my rib against the potholed asphalt. Someone must have called my brother, or he was noticing things from his side of his general store, because he came with that guy who sold phones, and they pulled us both up and took us to one of the textile stores. We sat there and were given water and gummy worms, which I sold at my store but had never eaten.

"What were you doing with the milkmaid?" shouted my brother.

"Nothing! Nothing at all! She had fainted! I was doing my best to help."

"And, is she okay? What is her health problem? Did you stop and consult a doctor before you thought to help? Did you forget that she is meant to be married? Married women are meant to be touched by their husbands and no one else."

My brother never asked her any of these questions. She was sipping her water on a chair by herself, but it was on the other side of the counter with the stacks of fabric underneath, and she could hear everything. I'd say something like, 'You find some excuse to talk to me like this almost every single day. Don't you have any respect for how much I lent you so you could start up your own store? Did you forget you're my baby brother, younger than me by almost seven years? Show some respect.' He'd apologise immediately, 'You're right, I'm sorry, but you know how high my blood pressure gets. I can't control it sometimes.' We'd hug for the first time in years, call the doctor, and figure out a way to help the girl together.

The call to the doctor never came, understandably, as it was expensive and he was far away. The milkmaid finished her water, and my brother tossed his paper cup directly out of the store and onto the main road.

"Can you escort her back home? We're all busy tending to our own stores at the moment."

"And I am not?"

"Your son is home. That's a luxury none of the rest of us have."

I was stuck in a predicament. I wasn't going to tell any of these other men that my son was useless, but I didn't want to lose sales. Ooh, another person's health was what I should have been focusing on, not my own material gains. I turned to the milkmaid and gave the same smile I gave to my customers, a winky one I saw on an advertisement many years ago.

"Dearie, I don't know if you heard, but…"

"I heard," she interrupted, but didn't say much of anything else.

"Fine," I said. "Let's go."

We went to my store and picked up my motorcycle. I didn't bother saying anything to my son; I just closed my door and locked it. The main road went on and on with all the different stores on both sides, until it reached a fork that then split off onto a dirt road and a lot of trails leading to more and more shacks. It wasn't all plains. There were plenty of banana trees, and rows of sugar cane, and rubber plants. The milkmaid wasn't saying anything to me. She was probably enjoying the view on our drive, while I was counting with my fingers how much money I would lose if I stayed out longer than twenty minutes.

"Fifty-seven."

"What?" the milkmaid asked.

"Sorry. I did not realise I spoke out loud."

The milkmaid should've said, 'That's okay, I do that too,' or 'Carry on,' or 'Why the number fifty-seven?' but she said nothing, and it made me feel bad, because I felt that when someone said something, it was polite to at least say something, anything, in return.

"My son..." I murmured.

"What?" she asked again. If I thought too much about my son, my heartbeat would get too fast. My hands were already shaking, and it wasn't safe to drive like that. I stopped the motorcycle.

"Why are we stopping?" the milkmaid asked. I was pretty sure she wasn't the least bit curious about my latest burst of self-talk, but I couldn't help myself. The words poured out.

"I was called into town, to go over the new stocks for the store, and I told my son, my smart and reliable son, to watch the store for me. It'd take only a few hours. He just had to sit there and help customers. But, oh, he couldn't do that. Why, how could he, when he had oh-so-many important messages waiting for him on his phone? Not to mention the big deal he is making over our television, which he broke, not me! *He* should be the one paying for it; *he* should be the one calling the repairman, but he can't, because he doesn't have any money..."

The milkmaid opened her mouth to say something, but I wasn't finished.

"He is going to be so successful ... he is a charming and intelligent boy with all the potential in the world... Yet all he does is complain! 'We're so poor! I need money! We're so poor! Wah, wah, wah!' And, then he spends everything on beer instead of books! He thinks I don't know, but my father was an alcoholic; I don't have to smell it on his breath to smell it on his sweat. He doesn't appreciate anything! His life, his school, his pathetic old man of a father..."

By now the milkmaid had found a big rock to sit on and was picking at a spot on her dress. I stopped speaking and let out two big sighs. I had the feeling that if I didn't get the rest of these feelings out, my eyes were going to twitch right out of their sockets. No, it was physically impossible for that to happen, but after some more sighing and pacing, the tension finally worked its way out of my back, and I remembered the milkmaid's health was at stake. We got back on the bike and continued our journey until we reached the giant fence that surrounded her father's estate, with its twenty cows grazing in the wild grass. My eyes were still twitching as I drove along the fence to her house. I was imagining my son back at the store. By now, he would be full of contrition as he realised that I must have been upset with him, or I wouldn't have left without saying goodbye. I could see it already: 'Oh, father,' he'd say, and he'd run to the door to meet me. 'I'm sorry I'm such a bad son.'

'I'm sorry too,' I'd say, and I'd hug him and kiss him on the forehead. 'I love you more than anything else in this world.'

It was all so beautiful, what was in my head, far from reality. I think I knew that I would return home to find him still sitting there with his feet up, listening to music on his headset, probably unaware that I had ever left the store. But while I was still riding my motorcycle, I was back in the fantasy, imagining the happy reunion of father and son, until I was jolted out of my daydream by a voice from the back of the motorcycle. I couldn't have imagined that the milkmaid would ever attempt to hold a conversation with me, so when she did speak up, I almost ran us into the bushes.

"What does honour mean for a woman?" she had asked me. A young person, asking me a question? My eyes lit up as they hadn't done for years.

"Honour is a very important thing, especially for women. It might be the most important thing, indeed. So many of you these days have no honour. The things you watch on your phones, the things you gossip about in front of your parents ... bleh! I am telling you, a woman with no honour is worse than a woman who is already dead. Such women do nothing for their parents but spit on their family's name. Do they forget how much parents have done for their children? I think all children who are willing to do anything to disgrace their parents deserve worse than death. No, they should be flailed naked and forced to walk on coals, or spikes! That way they can feel the shame their fathers feel over having raised someone who doesn't care about them ... that way they can repent!"

I had to stop the motorcycle again, I was getting that upset. I was seeing it all over again, my son, running out the door of our store, yelling, 'Oh, father, I'm so sorry I'm such a bad son.'

'I'm sorry too,' I'd say, and I'd hug him and kiss him on the forehead. 'I love you more than anything else in this world. Why can't you behave? Why can't you treat me well?' He'd say, 'I may be nineteen, but I'm a boy at heart. I love you, but I don't know how to express it. I'll pay you for all the damages I've done. I won't become a doctor, I won't work in finance; I'm going to come back to the store and take care of it, the way you dreamed I would — the way you did after grandfather dearest died.' I'd say, 'Oh, son!' and we'd cradle each other by the neck. It was a beautiful dream, but I was nowhere near my store; I was in front of the main hut of the cow estate. It was a two-storey brick structure with a thatched roof, and over by the fence was an elevated floor with a roof empty of walls, with a table and hammock and broken television screen, all colonised by the chickens. Beer cans and used condoms were everywhere, to the point that you couldn't differentiate them from the dirt. They didn't belong to the girl; I knew enough of that man she had to call her father to know that this obscene mess was his doing.

"You should pay someone to clean this place," I chuckled, but the milkmaid was once more like a ghost. She hovered off of my motorbike, gave the entire estate a forlorn stare, and moved towards her door. She looked back at me one last time. I didn't give her the winky smile. Instead I gave her the one where none of my teeth showed, but where my eyes did all the smiling. "Thank you for listening to me," I said. "It's nice to know there are some youngsters who listen to their elders."

She must have not heard what I said correctly, because she, too, slammed the door on me.

(The Convenience Store Owner)

"I guess I was wrong,"
I said out loud to myself,
driving back to the main road.

I am built from the clay of the spirits.
I stare at the eyes of the snake.
I do not back down.

"Children are children,
and I can't expect any more from her
than I would from my own child."

Then, why are you afraid of them,
these men who have the soft bark over their skin,
who wield blades and metal arrows?

I was going to tell him directly to pay for the television,
and if he was going to protest,
he could sleep at my brother's house,
until he went back to school.

I held my hand against the red bark of the tree,
to feel the charred earth against my skin.

I wasn't going to say anything else, I swore.
"My son is going to learn to behave."

I do not know if I am afraid, or worried.
Their spells used to cause our adults and children to fall
sick. The strange bend of their blades. The texture of their
skin. These are the things I know, but there is much I do not
know. They do little to scare me, yet I feel as if I have no
control.

The finger trees were far in the distance. The midday
sun used them like its eyelid, with the vines around them

(The Silencer)

the flittering of its eyelashes. The red tree's mark was a scratch. It was not the scratch of human nails, nor was it the scratch of the great cat's paw. It was a deep indent the shape of a crescent moon, thin, but wide enough to have eaten half of the red tree's width.

Such are the mysteries of the jungle. Perhaps, where the thatched man is, they control the great cats and ride them to their huts. They might have adapted the bark of their arms to allow them to hop between the branches. Or, they might have put their metal arrows so deep in the minds of the monkeys and turtles that the animals can no longer walk. These are the things I do not know. During these moons, I have seen that they have their ways to hurt the trees.

There was a path of pointed bush between the vines. The stubs of their roots were left, but not the bodies. I sniffed a foreign smell, but I couldn't make out what it was. It wasn't papaya, or sapota, or nuts, or turtle, or fish, or great cat, or monkey, or any other kind of flesh. If I even tried to breathe, it made me cough.

Do they possess animals or fruits that emit scents I cannot dare imagine?

I took the path away from the stump, taking care not to hit my head on a nearby wasp's nest, and slapping my palm against my mouth. These wasps were sensitive to noise. A family of monkeys sat on the roots on the other side of the nest. One of the children was walking to its mother with its rear up. The mother monkeys hissed at me through their teeth. I hooted and made passage. They did not bite. I leaned against one of the finger trees where there was a bush of red berries, and picked some to store in my satchel.

Do you remember the first time we ate these together?

I do, my dear wife, how the berries stained your lips, how I traced the juices down to your garland of bones, down to your breasts.

Eat them, for me.

I will not. I am hungry, but only for the turtle meat of our clan. I have wandered many a moon to reach the land of the thatched people, as I have traversed many falls and rises of the sun to return to ours. Do not be lonely. Do not talk to the spirits alone. I want nothing more than to see you. I want to eat from the berries together, as we do every half-moon. I will be home soon.

I was running again. I tapped my hands against the trees around me. The bark of the finger tree was coarse, but soft, while the drum tree was battered, but rough. Those bushes with thorns, those I did not touch. I was by the tree trunk the width of one man and the height of a hundred, the branches that flamed in all the directions at once, the type my family had lived in, far north of here, before our conquerors had come.

They are here, they are here! I thank the spirits that the trees remain here. The land of the thatched man is a land without trees. Or, rather, the land I discovered was a land without trees, a land where the bodies of the red trees were nothing but stumps.

Could it have been the plottings of the great cats or the monkeys?

Not at all. I have hunted every kind of great cat and tasted their meat and felt their pelt. I have studied the monkeys since the day I was born. These thatched men, they are taller, they attach things to their skins, and they have tools that we have never seen.

But, why would they tear down the red trees?

This is another thing about them I do not know.

I found a red tree and ran my finger along it. I walked until the sun closed its eye, the clouds curling over it. The sky was magenta, the sky was mauve, the sky was black. I crossed the river, to the side of our conquerors, to the side of my home. The orange water was darkened by the moss and tree branches and mud. The waves gurgled and guzzled and gulped.

There were corpses in the place of the mangroves, gutted of their intestines by the arrows. I waded into the water and began to swim. The clouds combined with the smoke from burning trees to form billowing shapes in the sky.

Had the thatched men already arrived?

I climbed up the silt. Outside of the first tent, one of the warriors who had found the first of these thatched men stood scratching himself. His skin was covered in red bumps, and there were patches of exposed muscle visible on his arms and legs.

"What happened? What did the thatched men do to you?"

He muttered an inaudible reply through the smoky night air, then began shouting and reaching out to grab at me. I could not let myself be touched. I saw the corpses of the wives inside the tent, every one of their bodies covered in the same red bumps.

There's a reason why some of these tents have been burnt to ashes. These bumps must not be allowed to spread.

I made flame with the flint and set fire to this tent. This warrior had never been a friend. He made my father dance on arrowheads while our land was being taken, and he used one of my cousins as a sex slave. He curled back his lips in anguish and groaned to their souls.

His suffering is deserved, but it brings no pleasure.

Where are you, my husband?

I am coming, my wife.

Her tent had not been burnt, and nor had the chief's. The tents in the jungle had also been spared. The inhabitants there appeared to live in normalcy. The children who were wearing the pelt of the thatched man were coughing in the tree branches. Some of the women were cooking the turtle meat under the flame, while others were napping in the silt. Everyone's breathing seemed shallow, uneven. I shivered into my love's tent. The sight of bruises over her body left me speechless.

"My love," she said as she opened her eyes. "You have come."

Why do you speak like that? Is it because you are hurt?

"Mhm."

"What did you find? What was on the other side of these trees? No, it does not concern us. The trees have been taken by them. Their spirits are aching. They have come to cry to me every moon. They do not realise that we are crying for our own reasons."

She, my wife, kneeled up to sit. I crouched down, pulled her into my chest.

In the arms of my wife, it is impossible to tell what is close from what is far. It is a place of its own, where the spirit can wander away from the body, where the only sound is her voice. No heart thumps as loud as the one lost in another's energy.

"I have administered every medicine on myself to assure that the sickness does not reach me. It is hard to tell whether or not I have succumbed."

I found the berries I had picked and fed them to her. The chief's son burst into the tent. His body was free of red bumps, but was covered in small cuts. He held out a pile of great cat meat, skinned of its pelt.

"You have come!"

"Shhh!"

"You have come ... You do not know how much has changed."

Yes, I can see that. The last time we trained, and we discovered a great cat, you fled behind my back. This moon, your shoulders and chest are covered in scratch marks, and you are proudly carrying its meat.

"There were members of the tribe who were fleeing. My father ... our chief ... he started killing them! He held up my grandfather's skull for everyone to see and said this was the tribe of the great conqueror, and that no one was meant to leave! No one! His warriors killed more people that moon than the disease!"

Is what he said the truth? My love peered into me, deep.

"Yes, what he has said has transpired. I was not made to look this way from the disease. I was made to look this way because the chief and his warriors took turns beating me. I told you already the spirits warned us to leave. Look how many bodies have succumbed to the disease. Tens of children have been buried under their tents, as have many of the wives. The ground of our tents is more corpse than skeleton. Many of our people are living with the bodies and becoming sicker. By the time the thatched men come, no one will be left alive. If the chief survives, I doubt his arrows will be able to pierce their skin."

I love you.

Why? You had the right to take any woman as your wife. You were the one who saved the chief. You were meant to be a slave, the remainder of a tribe whose traitors were long killed. Yet, when the chief was on his hunt for more land, it was not the warriors with their spears who struck at the pack of great cats. You killed each and every one of them with your bare hands. You could have had a whole tent full of women, anyone. It is a mystery to me and the spirits why you would choose the woman who screams, possessed by the spirits during the moon and the sun, scares little children, is cursed to never conceive.

"They are coming closer, with the passing of every sun. The spirits speak little of them. I do not know if they are our enemies; I saw the corpse before it was eaten. Once stripped of its skin, it was merely a different colour and height than our men."

I see them, you know, our children, the children I was never given, often with the spirits. I hear the spirits tell me the names they would have had if they were born. You should never have married me. Imagine the children you could have had with another woman. Imagine how happy you could have been if you weren't with me.

Lies. I did not believe that our children were taken as payment for the spirits she summoned. No matter how much black paste she applied to her skin, no matter how each and every bone in her garland shone, I had the deepest sensation in my ribs that the reason we could not conceive children had to do with a problem somewhere inside of me. It was my fault she was never a mother. It was all my fault.

"Nevertheless, the river will grow bigger. The hands of the waves will take us into its body and swallow us whole. There is nothing we can do about this. I believe the spirits have decided we do not deserve the land anymore. Oh, how our ancestors have warned us. Oh, how the spirits cry as death grows more certain."

So, why do I love you? Because you are the other member of this tribe who has lost everything. A child who was never raised by parents. A child who was taken by the previous shaman when she was a baby and forced to spar with the spirits in the banished lands. Of the children divined to be shamans, you were the one who survived. As did I. The men of this tribe shot down every one of my family. I was never circumcised, I was never addressed as one of this tribe, I was meant to be a slave. I became a man of honour through my deeds, but I will never forget the death of my parents, my cousins, my uncles, the men and women of my tribe. You were forced into rebirth, as I was in my own way. I was not any other man the way you were not any other woman. You and I are different. We find love in each other knowing we will find love in no one else.

I took out of my satchel one of the few flowers she liked. It was red, dirty around the stem, with small blue corollas, arched into the air in the form of a kiss. My wife took the flower with her bruised hand, held the crumpled petals.

People around you take you for granted, but you are everything to me. You are a leader, a fighter, everything a woman ought to be. You are the person I love. You are the thoughts I can never articulate. You are the reason why I believe in myself. You are the person who gives me faith, and who inspires me to live my life vividly. I can't imagine opening up to someone else the way I can with you. You're the only person in this world who is special to me.

I sucked on my saliva. Our eyes met.

As long as you keep your hand in mine, I can stare into the eyes of a great cat and never feel my heart shudder. With you near me, I can walk into the depths of this river and find my mouth full of breath. I can reach up and touch the sun and never feel as much warmth as I do when my hand is around yours.

I don't know if I will ever be able to say it out loud. Yet, I know that whatever I have never said has already been heard.

My hand gripped hers tightly, the flower crushed between our palms.

"Remember what I told you the moon before you left. Take the drink of the prophecies. The spirits have told me it is time. Thank you for touching me. Thank you for seeing the beauty that no one else would see in me. Thank you for your love. You know what you must do."

"Mhm."

I held the drink of the prophecies in one hand, carried the chief's son by the other, and hid them in the darkness, under the flaps of the branches, in the shade of the moon.

"What's going on? Where are you taking me?"

The clouds did little to tint the moonlight. The river rushed and roared, as did the sounds of the dragonflies, buzzing about. Plants the size of my legs hung against the mud cliff. I showed the boy that we must swim. Thus, we swam. The moon brimmed with the light of all the spirits. We reached the other side of the forest.

This is the land where the end of days was meant to begin.

We crossed through the mangroves, walked up the body of silt. In the pinches of silt, insects burrowed and left clumps shaped like teardrops in small trails. In the pinches of dark, the beetles and worms smashed against our toes. I stared between the vines, gave the focus of both of my eyes to the moon.

What the chief has done to you is unacceptable. A chief who harms the body of our spirits might as well have thrown the bones of his father into the water. He has no respect for the people of his tribe. He has no respect for the past or the future. I have seen the way he treats his slaves; it is no surprise that he treats his people the same. He cares most about his pride, and he will sacrifice every man and woman to the spirits if it means that he can please the eyes that stare from his corona.

We reached an edge of the trees where there were no footprints, where the roots clutched the earth like bony hands. The wind breathed, the breeze yawned. I threw the flask to the boy's feet.

"Drink."

"But ... I'm not ready ... but ... I'm a boy but ... I'm the chief's son ... I'm not meant to be the chief..."

I opened the flask of turtle shell and poured the sacred drink down into his throat. I covered his nose, forced him to choke. It did not take long. He was fainting, convulsing, vomiting.

No thatched man must dare conquer our land. You are the son of each and every man who believes in you as well as the son of the chief. The spirits have spoken. You will be the first to help our tribe reach the lands beyond the river. If you can make the great cats bow, you will be able to break the backs of the thatched men. You will do so respecting the needs of your people. You will treat them with care and dignity. This is why I trained you in these forests long after your father dismissed you as a girl. This is why I allowed you to play with the monkeys, learn of their ways, teach them how to use tools and make use of their space. This is compassion, this is mercy. This is nothing you learned from your ancestors. This is the gift from the spirits.

The spirits of the drink flung his body against the tree trunk, bruised his head with the blood of bark. The chief's son was shouting.

"I want to be a man; I want to be a man!"

A man you will become, indeed.

The spirits never visited me
on any other moon, except this one.

(The Silencer)

Twinkle, twinkle did the stars.

We have come on behalf of the shaman.
She is no longer responding to our voices.
Do you know where she could have gone?

I bet my tears looked fake, but not from afar.

I held the roots of the bushes,
tugged at their fingers.
I had no response.

For a narcissist better at stitching lies than dresses, it would have to make do. The first time I met this rag-stitcher who called herself a designer was at a gala similar to this one, maybe six years ago. Back then, her shtick wasn't about saving nature. She might as well have been vandalising it with the trash-bag shades she called fierce, but

(The Famous Singer)

I had a fashion show to introduce, and she was the It designer of the moment, and we both got something out of that. At the other few events where we ran across each other, we exchanged smooches and posed together for the paparazzi. It was something like what was happening now, only this time she was showing off her new line of seaweed bracelets. She fastened one of the bands to my wrist, fussed with it for a moment, and held it out for all the flashes. The flower dress she wore could have been made at the market on the other side of the Great Founder's Plaza for a thirtieth the price, but it was elegant in its own way. I could give her that much. It appeared to be made of real roses, probably imported.

"It's a dream to hold your hand again," she said. A paparazzo was leaning in, getting too close to my face, no doubt making my teeth glint like the headlamps of a car. I wanted to deck him the way my bodyguard did to my more stalker-y fans, but I resolved to be ladylike, and remembered what I was told long before I became a star — that boys liked it when you smiled, and didn't care about much else. Oh, I smiled. I made those teeth gleam brighter than diamonds, and I thanked the dear, I embraced her, with my neck relaxed, elongated, and my braceleted wrist dangling for the cameras. If I could touch all of those nasty men for all those decades, hugging this inconsequential flea of a woman was easy work. Not to mention that this angle showed off my wide shoulders, the stylish flow of my silver-studded couture, and, most importantly, the pearl necklace, gifted to me by the best designer of this land specifically for this gala.

The designer and I walked hand-in-hand, rotating around the flashes, making sure they got as many pictures as they needed. With one exception, they even managed to favour our good sides. When that failed, it was my mistake; I'd angled my body near the crystal punch bowl just as one of the paparazzi leapt from the other side to capture my backside. Wonderful, I thought, another not-so-flattering picture of everyone's favourite new pop singer with her derrière lit in this lace like a candle. It would be all over the internet by morning. Just thinking about how much my rear popped out of this dress was making me imagine all those hands on it, and I wanted none of that. I wanted to be a normal girl. Except, this normal girl wasn't a girl anymore; she was a star who happened to have a wide rear. Even when I stood straighter and held up the curve of my back more elegantly, my backside was the first thing that everyone noticed, and the main thing that defined my shape. I didn't want to think about it anymore, which was why I was smiling and humming again.

Do-re-mi-fa-so-la-ti-do.

This sweatshop worker playing designer-of-the-week was noticing one of the other musicians on the Top 40, who must have been contracted to advertise something of hers for some reason or another, because as soon as those paparazzi were gaining interest in some of the other celebrities entering the ball, she ditched me and went off to talk.

"Goodbye, dearie," she said. "I'll let you know when the next line launches, okay?"

A mass murderer could have said it with more charm in the voice. Did I break her bracelet off while she was walking away? Oops, guess she would have to scour the sea for some other plant to make clothes with. I had other people to talk to. Ignoring the one paparazzo who stuck around me, the only other person I could see was a former 'somebody' who had, over the last few years, become a nobody. She had released a single that won a lot of awards, but her album didn't do too hot, and she was having trouble writing songs for the next one. She was one of the first few singers who were there for me when I needed her, and I mean really there for me. We would be up in the studio, getting lost in the sound of each other's voices and singing our hearts out, and no one was recording us; we just happened to be around at the same time and wanted to have fun. We met all the time before I landed in the Top 40, but after I wound up on the A-list, everything changed. She started to ignore me, and I had the feeling that my success had something to do with why she was cold. I didn't want to believe it, because it felt like something a less mature artist would do. I thought she was bigger than that.

I walked between the tables where everyone was sitting. There were some conversations with this guitarist or that producer, but they were a bust. I only pretended to listen to them because the cameras were nearby and some of the snaps were going to look good for my agent. I gave my waves and blew my kisses, and I struck a pose with whoever approached. I finally found my girl, standing with some of the producers in a circle by the window.

"Dearest, how are you doing?" I exclaimed. Looking closer at her, I realised how much of a mess she was. I mean, she had a team of people to make her look good, like every other star in the biz, but the bags under her eyes were big enough to carry shoes, and her cheeks looked gaunt. Her skin was a little ashy, and I noticed that her elbows were dry and cracked. She was just off. Maybe she had something to say with me, but the window she and the producers were standing by happened to be on the other side of Galaxy

Mall, which was dominated by a giant billboard of me photoshopped into the wild, with rhinos and lions all around me and my eyebrows bleached blonde. Before my old friend could speak, the producers in her circle leaned in and asked a bunch of questions. They wanted to know when I was going to start recording the second album, who was working on it with me, and what they could do to make me an even bigger star. My friend was retreating onto a little private island of her own making. I turned to the producers and told them that my agent would be happy to answer their questions. That seemed to shut them down. I picked up a martini from the waiter and offered it to my old buddy, but it wasn't enough to get her to say what was on her mind.

"Thanks," she said, looking at me blankly. When I asked her what was going on, she said, "Just working on my next album. You know, it's just hard to deal with all these producers wanting you. Like, I get it, I'm hot shit, but I can't work with everyone; I can't sing with just anyone. I need to work with the people who are there for me. You understand, don't you?"

"I do," I said, but I really didn't know what she might be insinuating. "I mean, I'm there for you."

She gave a really loud groan, the kind you give when you have a lot to say but none of the patience to say it, and she made some lame excuse. I can't even remember what it was; that's how clearly made up it was.

"I really didn't do anything wrong," I said as she was leaving. "I don't know why you are mad at me."

I couldn't say anymore because the paparazzi had a second sense when it came to these spats between stars, and they were almost jumping over the tables to capture what looked like a sour moment between us. I didn't like giving these cheesy grins and waving happily when someone was actually mad at me, but then I remembered that I hadn't seen a person be real since I was about ten, and that all men and women were monsters, really, and that it just depended on how they wanted to eat their prey.

Do-re-mi-fa-so-la-ti-do.

Just then my phone rang, and I knew it was him. He seemed to know when I was trying to avoid thinking about the things he and his clients did to me, and he invariably chose that moment to call. I could have ignored him, but he always found a way to get back at me, like when I got onto the Top 40 the first time, and I thought I was a star, and I told my bodyguard everything, sure that he wouldn't be like the police, that he would listen to me, help me out. But the next night, he made his bodyguards and close clients lock me up in my bedroom. They tied me up so good I couldn't run, or stand. They used me for their fun. I didn't think I could stand another round with all of them, I didn't want my pet cat to go the way of my pet dog, which was why I pulled out a comb, my headsets, and an extra pair of stockings to get to my phone. It must have been a sight for all of these paparazzi to see a star empty her purse like that, in public. They certainly took their share of pictures as I stuffed everything back into my bag, then found a little corner in the white corridor outside of the banquet hall where I could pick up his call.

After all that mental preparation, it wasn't even him. I assumed it was because he disguised all of his phone calls with an unknown caller ID, but this phone number was actually unknown.

"It has been a long time, my bed-sister. How have you been singing?"

I gulped deeply. It was easier to gulp air than to speak when you were speaking with the other half of your own shadow.

"I see you are busy," she went on. "Are you going down on that slime from a bitch?"

No, I wasn't, but he had already delivered a handwritten message to my hotel room saying he was in the lobby, and that he wasn't attending the gala, but that the moment that the awards were given and I finished performing, he was going to come to room 809, he was going to pound on my door until I opened, and he and all of his friends were going to play with me.

"Are you still singing lullabies to yourself? Do-re-mi-fa-so-la-ti-do, I remember how you practiced your scales while they were clawing into your privates and spitting at you. I do not cast judgment on it. We were little girls, we all had to do what we had to do to survive. I don't know what other girls he sold out and about had to go through, because you were my bed-sister. You were the one who had to watch me be torn up by them, as I had to watch them violate you. It creates a certain bond, don't you think?"

I didn't think so. We were both sold by our parents to a pimp at the age of ten, to be drugged and molested and raped until we came of age, but we weren't alike in any other ways that I could gather.

"My father sold me because he had too many other love children to feed, and I really wasn't good at selling books on the road with only one arm."

Mine were told by him that I had a great voice, and he was a manager, and he was going to take me to the city, he was going to make me a star. He did do those things, but I didn't know I was going to be spending every day with twenty-plus men, without condoms, without a blanket, with only the one arm of the other girl he felt like selling to cuddle with me.

"You do have a pretty voice, I will admit. I knew it then, and I know it now. I've heard your song; you have gotten far. It's a shame that your success came at the cost of something you would have never wished to trade away. I believe it must be one of the worst feelings in the world, to feel like you owe a man who made you his toy. You must hate him, really. Isn't there a part of you that wants revenge?

The shivers in my spine were nails and scissors and knives.

"I am outside the Plaza Hotel, by the parking lot. He is waiting for you, and he is waiting for me. Come down and meet me. With your help, we can watch the slime guzzle down the sewer for the last time."

Was my phone low on battery, or did she hang up? I stuffed the device in my purse and looked around. It wasn't a hot time of the year, but I was sweating all over my bra. It was almost eight o'clock. In two hours, I would have to sing. It wasn't the wall's fault, for any of this, but I hit it anyway, the way I threw my fists at the first man he made me sit on until he poured a liquid down my throat and made the world go away. When I woke up, every organ in my body hurt, and blood was dripping from down there — so much blood.

Do-re-mi-fa-so-la-ti-do.

I did hate him, that was a hundred percent for sure. I just wasn't sure what I wanted to do about it. Or not quite. I wasn't taking the elevator; I took the stairs because they were less crowded, making it less likely that I would be spotted by a fan. When I got to the second floor, I allowed one of the maids to take some pictures with me, on the condition she would swipe me out of the exit for the staff. I got to the other side of the parking lot and looked around, searching faces. Eventually I saw her behind the first row of cars. She was nowhere near a dumpster, but the foam of filth that was on her clothing smelled as though she'd been living in one for a year.

"My bed-sister..." I said, and I couldn't say any more. The last time we met she was seventeen and had just thrown herself out of a window — that was how badly she wanted out. A one-armed girl was a fetish object for him and his clients, but he made no effort to find her. I assumed he thought she died from the fall, as that was what I had thought. I was obviously wrong. This phone call was not some prank from Looker; she was very much alive, but in some ways not. After having to deal with Looker, all of us got stuck in raggedy clothes. Some of us wore it in our heart, but she kept it on her skin. The blanket she wore as a dress looked like something Looker would have put on us, so it didn't surprise me to see her in it. Neither did her gait — a limp combined with a stagger — as she moved over to where I stood. The fall must have done permanent damage to her legs, her back, her body as a whole. The old elegance was gone. What made the limp odd was how little it came from her body; it felt like the work of demons using her as a puppet, moving her limbs up and down. I had called my friend's skin ashy earlier, but my bed-sister had skin that looked like a gust of the wind could tug it off. Most of her skin was discoloured or dusty, and parts of her seemed to have been eaten, or at least colonised, by bugs. "What happened to you? Where have you been living to look like this? Are you living in a place at all? You were so beautiful. I can't believe how you look now."

I could not tell if my bed-sister was heaving, or if the shadows clinging to something inside of her coat created an overall impression of a figure in mid-convulsion.

"I hear too many questions of too little relevance. We will sneak into the lobby the same way you came out. If anyone asks who I am, you tell them we are sisters."

"Will anyone believe that the two of us could be sisters?"

"People believe anything celebrities say, and you shouldn't care if they believe us or not. We are not sisters by blood, but the things we have experienced in confinement make us more than sisters. Our destinies are intertwined. Tonight, as that slime of a man falls, we will be observed as one."

I had kept the door open with a brick just in case I needed to go back in. As we walked through the empty corridor towards the side of the lobby, I couldn't help asking her questions.

"You're planning to end it? But how? What's your plan? I don't think this is a good idea. He's smarter than us, I know it. No matter what you've thought up, he's already thought three steps ahead. I don't want to deal with the cops, I don't want to deal with him, oh, I don't want to deal with any of it anymore. Why, why, why?" I screamed that last part, and she cupped her hand against my mouth to make me stop. It wasn't any sense of solace that calmed me; it was the smell of her aged sweat that was making me retch. It wasn't the first time I was in a situation where I had to smell it, either. It was what I'd smelled for over a decade of my life — men of all sizes and shapes who never showered, but made me suck them off. I hated it when people smelled; it made me feel like I was back in his arms, and for too long.

When we got to the lobby, I didn't have to look for longer than a second to notice Looker's silver suit against the gold flakes of the sofa, showing off his brown loafers as he crossed his legs, the designer sunglasses on his forehead, the silver studs on each of his fingers. I couldn't look at him for long; a crowd was suddenly forming around me, and fans were shouting about how much they loved my music, and asking me to sign their clothing and their bodies. Where did my bed-sister go? She seemed to vanish just as I was being pulled into the crowd. I was tall in these heels; I didn't have to look far.

"You slime from a bitch, it is time for your reign to end," I heard her shout. Her arm rustled inside her jacket. I heard two clicks and saw her raise her arm. She pointed straight ahead. In those first seconds, only four others were aware of the possibility that someone was going to be shot: me, my bed-sister, Looker, and the one receptionist who was dutiful enough to pay attention to the lobby instead of swooning over a star. Did I feel any excitement or intrigue, anger or longing, knowing that he was soon going to be dead?

No, because of the four people present, he was the most aware. He stood, spread out his arms like he wanted to take flight, and stared poison right into her eyes. Humans are more animal than we admit. The girl may have surrendered herself to the shadows, but I was raped right beside this girl. I knew who she was when she didn't have a shadow's claw digging into her soul. She dropped her gun. It took only a few seconds for the ushers to pounce on her, for the screams to sound in different parts of the lounge, for men and women to spring up the stairs or lunge at the revolving door. I thought I would be safe to escape in the crowd. I took both of my heels off and ran towards the stairs. There was a reason why he was able to curse us all. He was more than an average human being. He found me in the crowd in seconds, took me by both breasts, and nuzzled his chin into my cleavage.

"She is the most difficult bitch to deal with. I paid off the police a good amount to make sure she learns her lesson tonight. Thank you for your help. Your reward is coming after your performance."

Do-re-mi-fa-so-la-ti-do. He was gone.

"That slime from a bitch! Let me find that slime from a bitch!"

I heard it the first time because she was shouting it at the ushers, I heard it on the stairs and on the seventh floor because it had to resound in my ears. No one must have missed me, because I got back to the convention hall. I was asked if I was on a smoking break; they chuckled as if they didn't realise that downstairs, there had almost been a shooting. They would find out soon enough; the gala would be evacuated, I wouldn't be free, he would find a way to find me, make sure I was in his hotel, or some other room, and I would always be with him, inside.

We were all ants trapped in molasses, waiting for the men to squeeze our hearts.

People were staring, cameras were flashing. It was a chore to put on those stupid grins as I walked back in, said hello to passing artists, philanthropists, and businessmen, and waited for the chaos to pour from outside in. I took my place in front of the champagne table, listening to the tackiest music, watching them swoon around the disco ball and one other, like flies around the same spoilt milk. I was hugging myself, remembering how he would play with my breasts when they were as big as bee stings, touching himself, licking me everywhere, but I was smiling, smiling because after I got him to think I could have a future doing this, he made those calls, and it was the first time I had sung to someone who wasn't one of the girls, and he stopped what he was doing, to tell me that I sang well.

I wasn't normally so twitchy, but my crooked arm flew out as I imagined elbowing him in the balls. But it wasn't anyone's balls at all. I had shoved my elbow into the ribs of one of the waiters, who looked so young he still had chin hairs that needed to be plucked rather than shaved. He had been balancing a tray of champagne glasses on his head. They came raining down and splashed and crashed all over the floor. The clinks and clanks of the broken glass were not so loud, but we stars perceived it as a deafening crash. We crowded around the young waiter in a circle and watched him pick up the pieces.

"They hire the most incompetent help, I'm telling you," said one of the music producers to one of his friends.

"Yes, yes, I know, and they must be related to the owner, I'm telling you, because no matter how much they mess up, they always come back out."

The waiter must have heard them; he was reacting to them but was speaking to me.

"Sorry kindest, ma'am, I didn't see you over there, I—"

"Did you hear how he said it?" laughed the wife of the guitarist of the punk band The Rising Loaf. "Sorry kindest, ma'am ... He going go do speak like this now."

Her cohorts had laughs that would make donkeys hang their heads. Couldn't they feel a little bad? Whenever a boy with that much acne burst out red, it was something like a national tragedy, and he had the look in his eyes of a baby; he really wasn't old enough to be immune to such teasing yet.

"It's okay," I said, and I helped him clean. If the stud-spangled dress was going to be freckled purple with wine, it was better that it wasn't from the sweat of my own clumsy hands.

"Now, your dress gone done be ruin," he said, prompting more laughs from the men and women who happened to still be hearing him. The paparazzi had formed a group around the mess and were taking pictures of me cleaning as if it were a charity act. After having to deal with the reappearance of my bed-sister, I wasn't in any sort of mood to put on an act.

"Don't worry about it," I said. "It wasn't anything at all. This dress has lived through much worse than a wine stain."

Compared to anything else I had been through, a little wine was nothing. I had done my part to organise the broken glass onto his part of the tray; of course when people saw a star doing something, they aped my efforts and pitched in. I got up, and I thought I would do my best to wash my dress before the stain could set. I walked behind the table with the wine fountain, on my way to the bathroom. The waiter had his own work to do, but he was such a sweetheart — he put down his plate of wine glasses and picked up an empty one, which he used as to shield my mess from the cameras, and he walked by my side all the way to the bathroom.

"Thank you," I said. "You don't have to do this."

"I done gone should do it. I did done do the mess, I did."

I smirked.

"You're from one of the villages in the mountains, aren't you?"

"What gave it away?"

"Everything," I laughed. "Your diction, your accent, your words. It is nice. You never see such people in these parts."

He was looking down as if he were ashamed, but he lost a bit of it when he realised how much of my smile was coming from my eyes. People from the mountains were friendly, sweet, genuine, willing to smile whether they knew you or not. I knew that because my parents had been from there, and it was the part of this country I had grown up in. Neighbours treated you like their own daughter there, the fruits were freshly picked, and the dinners took hours to prepare, but we were an incredibly poor region, so, in retrospect, it was no surprise that my parents sold me with the genuine belief they were doing me a favour.

"This a stupid question," he said when we got to the bathroom, "but who are you? I know you got to be somebody famous because you here, but I am bad, bad, with celebrities, and you done seem real nice. So, I go on look you up on the internet later so I go know who didn't rip my ear up."

"Rip my ear up? I haven't heard that expression in ages."

He opened the bathroom door for me. I curtseyed with my dress the way the people in the mountains did at the start of their folk dances, and he guffawed. You never saw boys with heart, or, you never saw them grow into men. I should have given him an autograph or something, but I had nothing to write it on. He wrinkled his eyebrows and pursed his mouth, wondering why I was paused for so long.

"This isn't ... ain't ... no fairy tale," he said. He was definitely exaggerating the lag because he knew I liked the way he talked. "I'm ain't not go learn your name not talking like this."

(The Famous Singer)

We certainly weren't close enough
for me to tell him that he,
a twenty-something from a village,
was the first person to make me forget who I was.

Grown-ups were tough like that,
not wanting to say anything ever to someone young,
thinking you had to be this age or that age to get it.

I gave him my hand for a shake,
let him hold it for however long he wanted,
along with the truest version of my smile,
or, rather, nothing much of a smile at all.

Did they forget the Incident,
when they wanted to lie to us?
How could they cover up death?
It was all around us.

"I don't think I need to be anyone for you.
I like being known as the girl who didn't 'rip your ear up.'
That's a good enough name, for now."

Whatever. Death affected us all.
I remembered when I was ten, around my baby sister's age
now, and we had a little puffy poodle named Bubbles. All
you had to do was push your hand against its head, and hair
would come out like cotton spores. Bubbles died because

(The Magician)

she found a chocolate bar. My father was supposed to be paying attention, but he was as much a phone addict then as he is now, and he wasn't looking at anyone or anything, he let the dog eat whatever, and we kids paid the price. My sister was just a toddler when our poodle and I suffered. Her goldfish may have died, but I wasn't going to watch her sleep with an empty fishbowl every night. Mommy called it lying, because I took that goldfish covered in white mold floating around the bubbles on the top of the bowl and threw it into the toilet, then made her drive to the nearest pet store between the hours of six and eight so we could buy a newer Mr. Fisherfish. Didn't they keep forgetting I was a magician? If I could pull coloured ribbons from a top hat and make my pet pigeon appear out of my armpits, why couldn't I take my sister's bowl into the bathroom, sprinkle a little magic dust into the water, and give the new one a magic kiss before returning all of it to that place under the curtain by her bed?

By the time I had finished, it must have been around nine, breakfast time, because the smell of diced potatoes was spreading through the house, and the steam from the tea kettle was snaking into the corridor, and I could hear a guest from downstairs. He was speaking so funny, he had to be our uncle from the capital who wrote articles for the newspaper. All of us could speak the national language. I didn't get why he was trying so hard that even the neighbours in the cottages next door could hear his gruff voice, slurred sounds, and mistakes. They were peering from their windows while I was going down the stairs.

"Wake up your sister!" Mommy shouted from the kitchen. "We don't have a lot of time to eat breakfast today."

I went up to the top banister and bellowed, "Hey, Sis, wake up!" Mommy shouted from the kitchen, "That's not going to wake her up," and I hollered back, "It will, I know it will." I went to the dining room and buttered the toast and got jam all over the stained glass, which Mommy should have covered up if we had guests, and shouted at her, "Why aren't we spending more time eating?" My father told us, "No shouting at the table." Then, he looked up from his phone, and then he looked up at me, and then he looked at the guest, and I looked at the guest, too.

Over the last year, Uncle Journalist had come to our house once a month and acted like a different person every single visit. The first time we met was during a magic show of mine. He had a lot of bushy hair, and he kept trying to speak our language without knowing how to say a single thing. The second time was after we all had to meet at some auntie's place, and he came wearing one of those plaid shirts that the aunties from here force children like me to wear, which he never took off, because he was wearing it still. Then, he kept coming over and over to those gatherings, and then he started coming over and over again to our house. Once, he and my father got drunk way past the time I was supposed to be sleeping, and he clucked at my father that he wasn't a chicken so loudly you could hear it all the way from the second floor, and he was threatening to finally find his mother's place and make it into a bachelor pad, and they sang folk songs until sunrise. The fourth or fifth or sixth time I don't remember, because by that time he was looking more like an uncle and less like a stranger. I remembered last week he came with his curls cut, which had made Mommy smile for a good hour and compare him to his grandfather. Today he was back to looking like a magician, missing the handkerchiefs in his tuxedo, a little more stage mystery in his green eyes.

My father and Mommy and Uncle Journalist must have long finished eating, because the plates for me and sister were the only ones left out, and their teacups were no longer steaming. Mommy flipped me some eggs for my bread and said, "Eat quickly, we are going on a family outing." I asked, "Where?" Mommy looked at Uncle Journalist and said, "We're finally finding your uncle's grandfather's house."

"Did you finally lose that bet?" I said, winking at Uncle Journalist. He tried to smile, but he wasn't good at it; his face just crumpled into a wrinkly ball. Then, Sis was yelling, "Hey! Hey!" from the second floor of the rails, waving into the dining room. Mommy looked up at her and told her, "Come down, now!" Sis tossed her hand in the air and pretended to flap her ponytail, much like how a diva would, and said, "I'm talking to him. Come up here this instant, Mr. Magician!" She curled her finger out, pointed at me, her legs as straight as the banisters themselves. I came up because I couldn't hide forever. Once we were in her room, she sat me on the floor by her bed, where her bowl was, shaking the bowl in my face.

"Who is this fishie?" Sis asked. I saw a live and healthy goldfish with a red flowing tail and said, "It's Mr. Fisherfish." She shook the bowl again and soaked my dirty socks with water. "Nuh-uh! Mr. Fisherfish isn't red, and this fish is way too fast." Her fish also wasn't that smart, or it wasn't that her fish was dumb, but slow, and I forgot how it was his trademark to stare at whoever was feeding him and wait almost a half hour before going for any of the flakes. He was also orange, and I should have paid attention to details like that, of course. I didn't have any more time to stare at that fishbowl, because Mommy interrupted us. "You'll have to eat your breakfast in the car. We're getting late." She pulled

Sis down regardless of what she had just said, and must have been forcing her to eat. I went back into my room and changed. I felt like the biggest fraud on this side of the lake, wearing my top hat and my black cloak, but I promised to myself I would wear it every day since I turned sixteen, and I wasn't going to stop doing magic, even on a bad day.

After she ate, we all got into the car, where Uncle Journalist asked me, "Magic, yours improve?" and I slapped him on the ear, pulled out a paper flower, and said, "Yes, much better, it is." Mommy clicked her tongue at me from the front seat, but I wasn't making fun of him; it was good to have someone to talk to, since Sis wasn't talking to me at all. I pulled a coin out of her ear and gave it to this uncle, and she crossed her arms around her stuffed rabbit more firmly. Uncle Journalist clapped his hands and inspected the coin, more interested in the face on the front. "No coin of this at capital," he said, and I told him, "Because it's sixty years old, and it's not a coin from there, it's a coin from here." He felt it up. I looked from my side of the window out. The roofs of the cottages were dinting against the clouds and making pewter out of the colours of the day. We rolled down the hill of our subdivision and onto the highway. It didn't take long for us to see the lake on the other side, the maple and aspen leaves littering the sides of the hill, and the lanterns from the autumn festival which had drifted from the boardwalk and stilled in the moss.

"Are we going to the festival?" Sis and I both shouted, but Sis shut up the moment she realised I had asked too. Mommy shouted, "No, I told you that we are going to see a cottage first," and she shouted at my father next, "Hey! Don't you realise you are driving? This is not the time to look at your phone," and my father, who never shouted, said in his grumpy voice, "Am I not allowed to look at my phone for directions, or do you expect me to teleport us to the place?" We turned at a place where one of the cypress trees was being used as a mark in the road, and we were by the lake, but on a pebble road, which was making us bump up and down the way you do when you ride a horse, alongside all the mansions that had statues in the shapes of mermaids, steps made out of marble up to the doors, but the millets were tall enough to be gates, and the walls were crushing into themselves. They stopped the car at one of the houses, and Mommy told us, "You both stay inside."

I came out anyways. We were standing in front of a giant house made of stones, which must have had stained-glass windows, but one had fallen out and shattered all over the front, and there were boards nailed all over the door. Uncle Journalist pulled at the boards over the door, but Mommy was catching him by the arm. She said, "It's not safe, you don't know what lives in that house now, and you don't know what will make it collapse," and Uncle Journalist said, "I don't care. I need to see what's inside." Uncle Journalist and my father ended up going under the planks, and they were in the house for some time, and I wanted to go in, too, but if Mommy grabbed Uncle Journalist by the arm when danger was near, she practically wrapped me into her shawl, pushed me into her like a mummy into a coffin, and shouted, "Don't you dare go in there!" I looked at my sister, playing alone with her doll with the window up. Son, I thought in the voice of my father, you made one promise too many out of magic, and it cost you your sister. I pulled some paper flowers out of Mommy's ear, but was thinking it was time to retire the trick handcuffs.

They came out, and we all drove. Mommy said, "Why don't we all go to the festival?" I let Sis scream, "Yeah! Yeah!" wanting to say the same thing, but not wanting her to feel like I was going to say it over her. No one was talking, but we drove onto the highway, not for long, because we reached the row of houses on both sides that must have been painted golden and white in the last month, because they were brick buildings before the Incident. It was a lot less crowded than usual. No one here was a tourist; they were all people clearly from here — the plaid shirt and dress pants for the men, the shawled heads and conservative wear for the ladies. I was surprised that my control freak mother wanted to be anywhere near the lake in the first place. I didn't care if a bomb had gone off; this was the autumn festival, and these aunties or uncles got it. They were eating flaming chocolate by the vendors and taking pictures with the men who were in their bear suits or pretending to be sages from another time period, because this was the only day which was meant to be merry in our town no matter what happened on any other day of the year. The live music was loud where we parked. The first performances were of traditional folk dances with the men and women wearing costumes. Some rock group that was famous here was reuniting for the first time since well before I was born. The lead singer was saying something on the speaker: "The Incident took some of our lives, but at least it gave the three of us a reason to write songs." That got a lot of applause, and Mommy agreed. During our walk to the boardwalk, she said, "This year has been quite tough on us, but I'm glad to say, this festival is the one thing that hasn't changed."

On our walk to the boardwalk, my father was swerving his phone to make the balls on the other side of the screen move, which earned him a slap from her. "You and your damn phone. I swear, if you kept your eyes on your own children instead of that thing..." On and on they went, and if Mommy was ten degrees less devout, she was going to take off her shawl and whip him. The planks of the pier wobbled and creaked. I bet if a fat man walked onto it he would break through and get dumped into the lake, or if dolphins and whales lived in fresh water, they could burst through the planks and give the old ladies heart attacks. If Sis was talking to me, I would have told her these things, and she would have laughed, but she was holding Uncle Journalist's hand, and they were looking sullenly at the water. Sis wanted to play the arcade games, and Uncle Journalist hadn't done it since he was a boy, so he went along with my father. I was a little too old to play those things, so I stood with Mother. A lot of people were walking by, old and young, skinny and fat, with baby strollers or lunchboxes, or with baseball caps and fanny packs, while firecrackers exploded in the distance, and some families on the other side of the lake were pushing the lanterns into the waves.

"Stay close to me," Mommy shouted, and pulled me by the ear. "They are coming back soon."

Sure enough, a few minutes later they skipped along from the other side of the grass, with Uncle Journalist holding Sis in one hand and a new giant plush pink rabbit in the other. Sis was so happy to see our father she tore the bunny out of his hands and showed it to Mommy. "Look what Uncle got me!" "It's beautiful," Mommy said, kneeling down and inspecting the thing for holes or insects. "He will certainly make a great night companion after a long wash." "Great job!" I said to Sis, and I gave her a thumbs-up, but she hid her face in her rabbit.

"They're going to start lighting the candles soon," Uncle Journalist said. He saw that I was staring at him, and he gave me the same thumbs-up I had given to Sis. I shuddered from how corny it was. We walked towards the pier where the banners pointed. "Can you believe this lake reeks still of waste?" Mommy complained. "Unbearable." "We're going to be smelling it here for the rest of our lives, so you better get used to it," my father said. Mommy tried to slap his phone away, but his reflexes were too quick. "I won't," she said. "I grew up around a place of beauty, and for me, it should always be that place." Uncle Journalist was beginning to smoke.

"Do you believe that if I haven't found what I've been looking for, I should leave?"

"First you have to tell me what it is you've been looking for," my father said.

"I don't know. Other than writing my article, I didn't have any expectations when I came here. I thought it would be another tragedy-stricken place like the ones I have covered before. But then, people invited me to their homes, and I grew closer to them, and the words of the language started making sense to me, and I thought, maybe if I could find that house, maybe it would mean something. But, well, you saw how the house looked. And to be honest, I felt more than bare when I was inside."

"Well," Mommy interrupted, "as I said earlier, you can stay at our house. You can write all the articles you want in the room upstairs, and for free." I whistled to signal a "No," as living upstairs would mean him getting my room and me sleeping with Sis. I shook my head at Sis, too. Instead of snickering or pushing me playfully, she made a giant stomp.

"I don't know if I feel comfortable with that."

The family in front of us was leaving, giving us a view of the lake. As they departed with their giant cotton-candy cones and pink fuzzy clothes, we could see the hills on the other side reflected in the water, and the fog riding through the distance like boats.

"Well, I think it's difficult to know what we want," my father said. "It's like a bear figuring out what fish he likes best. I think the emotions happen, and then you do something else, and you feel more of that emotion, and you keep on that track, but even on that track, you'll feel bored or sad. You get used to it, just like you get used to this emotion, or to a place."

Uncle chuckled. Mommy pulled herself into Father's shoulder and said, "Finally, you're giving great advice." I wouldn't say I was impressed, but it was funny how the little bald man who hunched over his phone could spread out his body like wings and open himself up to people he barely knew, but never gave advice like this to his kids, who needed it once in a while.

"I wonder if I am one of those people born to be eternally homeless," Uncle Journalist continued.

"How can you say that when it's been so long since you've been home?" Mommy asked.

"You mean this place, or the city where I work, or—"

"I mean, where you and your father and your mother lived. Your home."

Uncle Journalist folded his arms.

"That place is definitely not my home."

"How can you tell until you've been back?" Mommy asked. She took his arm. "As a mother myself, I implore you. Go home." Uncle tightened his lips. My father was better at being diplomatic. He rubbed his cousin's back. "I know it was hard for you, being called a sand-face or a half-breed growing up, having your mother doing what she did. But I think what my wife is saying is worth considering. A lot has changed in the last few decades. You might be surprised at what you find."

My father held out his phone with a half-smile.

"To family," he toasted. Mommy held out her lipstick.

"To family," she said. Uncle held out an unlit cigarette.

"To family," he said, and they broke into another conversation. This was how adults had conversations, got into arguments, made up, and appreciated what was between them. I didn't get it. I was sixteen, but still not anywhere close to an adult. We were passing a booth where a fortune teller was working. I waved my fingers and pinched Sis's bunny. "Stop it," she said. 'Stop it' was better than nothing. I kicked away one of the bottles she almost stepped on. We were progressing through the crowd the way ants fought against other ants. "Why aren't you talking to me?" I asked. Sis shook her head so hard her ponytail frazzled. "You know why, you know why, you know why."

Fair enough. "It wasn't right for you to treat Mr. Fisherfish that way." Sis pushed her plush toy into me. "He was my pet, and if he was gone, you should have told me. I'm not nine anymore." She was ten.

We came to an open part of the shore where a lot of people were standing, and the little children ducked down by the water, pushing small lanterns into the lake. It was something my grandfather and my great-grandfather and his grandfather had been doing every autumn festival. Even if it was a little smelly, the water looked how it did any other year, pebbly and pale. Not to mention if the lantern made it to the centre, it was said that whatever you wished for would come true. That was a risk worth taking for most of us who didn't have other kinds of help. Most of the lanterns were handmade, crafted in some of these tents, and so they fell apart the moment they got too moist. With how most of the kids were pushing them, it was their destiny not to make it far. Still, there was a line of thirty or so people waiting to have their shot at changing the stars.

"I think we can skip this event," Mommy complained. "Going anywhere close to that water these days isn't safe."

"Come on," my father said. "My cousin has seen only tragedies, let him see what makes our homeland unique."

"I can see it from here," Uncle Journalist said. "I don't like big crowds anyways. So, we agree to skip?"

"Wait," I said. "I am going to do this with Sis." Mommy took me aside by the shoulder and said, "Don't you even think of putting your hands at the water. Just give the lantern to that man over there helping the other children. He has gloves on, so he will do it for you. Now, we will treat your uncle to the bread puffs. Do you remember that stand? It was by the fortune teller." I said, "I do. We'll meet you there." Sister wasn't happy when they walked off. She said, "No fair. I want to eat bread puffs, too."

They were quite tasty, rolls of unleavened bread that puffed at their sides, and you could top them with marmalade or chocolate. I distracted myself with the clouds in the sky. One was like a man eating a doorknob, and another was a dented television remote, and another was a rabbit. I made a shadow puppet with my hands, but Sis crossed her arms around her plush toy. A child dipped his fingers into the lake to try to catch a shoe that had never been cleaned out, and he got slapped on the back of the head by one of his grandparents. I pointed at it and laughed, but Sis looked away and made her pout. I remembered we needed at least one lantern. I talked the teenager behind me into giving me his. He was quite direct that he needed this wish to pass his entrance exams, but I gave him a significant wad of cash my father had given me earlier for snacks. The air had changed. I relaxed in the misty cool of the early noon and in the heat and light of many small candles.

"We made it," I said.

"Hmph," my sister said.

"Let's make a wish."

I took off my gloves and took out a lighter from my jacket. I closed my eyes and flickered the flame and made the candle burn. I burnt my hand a little dropping the candle into the lantern. Sis smiled like it was my just deserts. She watched me from the foot of the line as I walked onto the shore. The grey pebbles and algae stuck to my boots. I centred the lantern on an incoming wave and pushed it and blew as the lake took it away. I stood up and watched the lantern bob around. I walked Sis back to where everyone else was eating. I left the lakeside because I didn't want to watch the lantern sink, or its candle to be doused.

"What did you wish for?" Mommy asked me. I replied, "For my sister to be my best friend for the rest of my life."

It didn't take long for my wish to work its magic. I wasn't a grade-A magician, but I didn't have to be to do what any good brother could do — turn bad memories into good ones. Sis still didn't talk to me until after we left the lake, but she let me hold her hand, and when she finally broke her silence, she asked me, "I think Mr. Fisher-Brother-Fish is a good name for our new pet, don't you agree?"

Our Ascent

Why, you dear little kumquat, my sister's dear eldest brat, whether you liked it or not, your cheeks were still shrubby with prepubescent hair, and you may have been angry because I called you out for what you were, a little boy begging for luxury cars and the globetrotting lifestyle of a man from a much richer country, forgetting your background in a metropolis where even the rich make less than the middle class of the first world, and so your eyes angered, sparrowed, and flew to the third-rate phones or cameras or contraptions for sale at this market, looking as far away from your aunt as possible because of a passing comment she had the right to make. You did not pay the taxes; your father did. You, in fact, earned too little for what you've demanded from him and my sister. You should have been grateful that you had someone who took you to these bargaining traps or slum-side tourist sights, places that would make your parents faint if they knew you had sojourned there.

"My dear, do you earn your own income?" I went on. "Do you live in your own house? Do you wash your own clothes and tidy up your own room? Well, if the answer to all of these is no, I am afraid that you are not yet an adult."

I stood up from the bench where we had been served and took out my purse. According to the menu above the vendor's head, it was 80 cents for a simple orange juice, 1.60 in total for the two we had, 1.50 for a mango and guava delight, and 2.50 for the coconut milkshake, and then I was going to buy some oranges for my own mother. Flipping through my wallet, I had about eighty, divided into a fifty and three ten-bills. The ten would suffice. The lady was busy serving another customer, my view of him blocked by a stack of melons. The smell of the cut coriander wafted from the vegetable section, and the mist from the ice used to make smoothies covered the countertop. I buttoned up my white fur coat and sipped my drink. The market was not really cold enough to justify a fur coat, but Mother told me that a young lady ought to choose elegance above all. Moreover, this advice extended beyond clothing and into conversation. I was coached to keep my speech smooth and inoffensive, for a young woman never knew when sharp words uttered in a moment's passion might come back to bite her. I tried to channel these teachings as I pursed my lips at my nephew, who stood near me, wiping the dust from his glasses.

"I can't believe I'm someone who gets all of her money from her husband and spends it on fur," I said, repeating the words I had overheard him say about me when he was on his phone, talking to his friend or girlfriend. I slapped him with my jacket.

"I think after a certain age, you are allowed to indulge yourself."

Meanwhile, I was going to spend more on the two of us today than I had spent in the last week. The vendor returned, and I asked, "My good lady, what would be the price for a bag of oranges?"

She looked at the stack in front of her and weighed as many as could fit in a bag and told me it would cost about three-fifty to four. This was one of the few delights of coming to the market: the prices were almost tragically cheap. Four plus 1.60 plus 1.50 plus 2.50 would be 9.60, and I could give the dot forty in change as a tip. The lady looked at the ten bill I had given her.

"No, no, this is not enough. It should be fifteen."

I was so incredulous that I chuckled. I pointed to each of the prices and voiced them out loud. She wasn't going to believe my math, so I finally took out the calculator on my phone and showed her the total price. That didn't help either. The woman made a damsel in distress face.

"Nephew, let's go."

We stood up. The bench was taken over by a woman with a basket of eggs and her child wrapped to her back with a scarf. Mother and baby were both covered in grime, and the child sneezed all over me. I moved my scarf from my mouth to tell this woman goodbye. "Anyways, I don't think I am spoiled," I said, though no one had openly accused me of such. I almost added that if I were spoiled, I would not even come to the market, but that was nothing I would say in such a public space.

"Hmm," my nephew said, lifting one eyebrow and scanning me up and down as if to say, "look at yourself.' The noise of the meat vendors killing their clucking chickens destroyed any possibility of conversation. It was for the better, frankly. I was not in the mood to have a young man half my age elaborate all the reasons why he considered me spoiled. Did he think because he said at every family gathering that he would never pick his career based on its salary and dressed himself like a lost musician that he was humble? He was certainly not as lower class as he wanted to seem. The smoke from the frying corn-on-the-cob made him recoil. As it rose to his face he started breathing through his hand and pinching his nose. I held out a handkerchief as he complained about how much the market had changed during his lifetime.

"I'm telling you, this used to be the best place to go if you wanted some cheap rice and eggs. It's gotten expensive in the last few years. All these tourists…"

Again, he was speaking of an experience that I doubted he'd had. He was twenty-one, a baby. Unless he started going out with his friends in high school, which my sister would never have let him do, he would have begun to visit this market a mere year or two earlier.

Oh, it was unbearable to walk on concrete that was almost slush because of the mud. I had to clutch my purse. Between the stands where telephones were unlocked or at the tarp under which suits and dresses hung in plastic bags, women sat on their buckets selling fermented drinks, their children feeding at their breasts, and men who carried bottles of alcohol publicly and wore shirts with logos of brands from decades ago.

"Do you always have to walk so fast?"

"Perhaps you are the one who walks slow," I said. Of all the days that my sister and her husband had to visit their paternal family in a town many hours from here, today the sun shone with a tropical heat, and I, expecting the typical clouds and smog and wind, was dressed in a scarf and jacket. Changes in weather brought out the worst in me: bumps, ulcers, and an irritable mood.

We came to an exit from the market that led onto a side alley towards the plaza. As I fumbled in my purse for my phone to call the driver, I bumped into someone's backpack. He was clearly a foreigner. He had our skin colour, but he had one of those backpacks that was taller than him, and he was paying more attention to his map than to his surroundings, a mistake no local would make. The other dead giveaway is that he was dressed in khaki shorts. Only backpackers wore those.

"My apologies."

The backpacker stared at me as if heavenly light was shining onto my head. He touched my shoulder, showing me his map and speaking quickly in a language so global I felt embarrassed not to understand. My nephew was looking at his phone. He was never the kind to socialise, as proven by how little he talked to the guests whenever I threw socials. I, however, liked that this man saw me as something more than the dull housewife of a corporate vice president, and I didn't want anyone, foreigner or local, to be pickpocketed or mugged.

"Founder Plaza, us, go, together," I said.

We crossed the market diagonally. Sizzled pigs dangled from rope, their empty eyes seeming to watch over us. The smell of fish was strongest near these exits, where the vendors slapped down slabs of fleshy trout and ordered us to take a look. I had to use my scarf to cover my nose. My nephew noticed the iconic musician on the front of the backpacker's shirt.

"Hey!" he said, and he crossed his fingers in the way of that celebrity. The tourist said his name, my cousin exclaimed some lyrics to a song, and we all had a good laugh. The tourist was excited and said a lot. My nephew, with a conversational level in this language, spoke a lot. I smiled. I felt a little less spoiled than my nephew had accused me of being and a little more adventurous than my relatives assumed, and I was genuinely thrilled at how my nephew was opening up to someone. I couldn't help but want to forgive him for judging me earlier.

We came to the plaza. Buses and shuttles were halted in traffic on the other side, and in the hustle and bustle of the pedestrians crossing whichever way, homeless men and women dotted the cobblestones. I was entranced by the stare of a woman who had collapsed by the steps leading up to the Great Founder's statue. She was wearing a brand of jacket I had seen once in my mother's closet, and a blanket draped over her legs in a manner that was flowing and somehow reminiscent of silk. She didn't beg. Her pupils and posture looked clear of the influence of alcohol and drugs, and she didn't cling to anyone's legs with her one arm. What affected me most were those miserable eyes that bore the suffering of a thousand lifetimes. She had bruises all over her body. I wasn't a doctor, but they looked new.

My nephew pointed the backpacker towards one of the country's finest archeological museums, and the backpacker slapped his forehead. It was a gesture I never understood, why someone would hurt himself for the sake of a revelation. My nephew showed his youth once more. A proper adult of our culture would have insisted the foreigner come for a meal with us, offer accommodation if a bond was felt, at least give a number in case he got lost or needed aid.

"Go accompany him to the museum," I said. "Call me when you finish. I will be by the statue."

My nephew grudgingly echoed my words, the backpacker gave two thumbs up, and I waved goodbye, giving him the business card of my husband should he get lost again. Now, had it been such a good idea to wait by the statue? Without clouds, I would need a parasol to withstand this heat. However, a parasol would be relatively costly in the plaza.

"Cigarette?" asked a man who was watching me. He was a bald and tan thing from another nation, perhaps one where men wore shirts that revealed their breasts. "What do here?"

Can you believe that he rubbed my arm? He patted me as though I was the tail of a cat, and he looked at me like I was one of the girls who wore fancy jackets and strutted around the plaza. Come to think of it, I was wearing a fancy jacket.

"What you do here? How much you want? How much you ask?"

He stepped close enough that our chests almost touched. I shoved his hand away and recoiled from the smell of his strong deodorant, and the rancid hamburger cheese on his breath. He slapped the hand that slapped him. I was going to find a policeman or a nice hooligan who would be willing to knock in his teeth. He had no elegance, this man. He was whirling his hands at me, grabbing for whatever part of my body he could.

"No, no, no leave."

He grabbed my hand and pulled. I'd had enough. I twisted his arm over his back as I was taught in self-defense class. He screamed and cursed in his own language and twirled around me on an axis. His fat was bulging out of his shirt. A beggar boy jumped up and down next to his legless mother and laughed. One guy stuck in traffic rolled down his window and took a photo with his phone. Some tourists took photos, too. The guy was reaching with his other arm and shouted for the police. I would not dare let him escape my grip. The boundaries of respect weren't set in stone like the laws of arithmetic, but there was still a set of norms that had been passed down for centuries. One of them was that it was never appropriate to touch a stranger, woman or man, without consent.

My arm was getting tired, particularly as I was also holding the bag of oranges and my purse, so I threw him onto the street. He was lucky one of the passing motorcycles didn't hit him.

"Fuck you, whore," he said. He made a lewd expression with his fingers, but I was more concerned that the oranges had been squashed. Nope, they were as firm as skulls. This sad excuse for a man scurried off. A few men and women were looking at me with starstruck eyes, but I was in no mood to give autographs. I bumped into some people who were waiting for street food. I kicked a rock so hard I could have broken my toe. I had had one good experience with a foreigner, and one bad one. I had become violent in a way my coach had never instructed me to be. I got pleasure from imagining kicking this man, in the knees, in the groin, and insulting his father, his mother, and the country of his birth. I sat down at the steps to the statue and took off my fur coat.

"Well, if romance is in the air."

I turned with fury but saw this one-armed woman looking at me. She lay over the steps and rested her head on a step, staring upwards.

"You saw what that man did to me?"

"I've seen what every man in the history of manhood has done to women like you."

I fanned my hands in the heat.

"Men like him are a real disgrace."

"I've known worse," she said. She was suddenly by me, and I was paralysed by her jaguar glare.

"I used to love seeing women hate men, until I learned that there is more to hatred than we can ever understand.

You're not the first or the last to be treated that way. Some women are picked on, others are beaten and violated. There are young girls sniffing glue by the city's port who get picked up in cars. They will never be able to erase the memories."

"You're right," I said. I swallowed. "Being hit on is nothing compared to what happens to those poor girls."

I peeled one of the oranges meant for my mother and offered some to her. She took one of the slices and cut the seeds out with her nails.

"You look like someone who has been through a lot," I said. "I apologise for that."

"Everything in this world is relative. I can never have your life. You will never know mine. There are rich businessmen and lawyers living a few blocks from the mall who will never know the pain of either of us. The point is that anyone alive or dead has the potential to hurt you. Even members of your family and trusted friends will take advantage of you when they see how easily your eyes forget."

I didn't feel like I had such enemies in my family, but I nodded along.

"It's important to snuff out your enemies when you have the chance. I had my chance, and at the end of it all, I couldn't do it."

She stared upwards, with eyes empty of emotion, her mouth cringed between a frown and a smirk. There we were, surrounded by people, yet somehow alone, baking in the sun. I could feel the heat on the hairs of my arms and the tip of my nose. I wanted to close my eyes and rest, but I was so compelled by the pain in her eyes that I could only stare.

"What's wrong?" I asked. She said nothing. "Do you wish you had taken your chance?

No, I saw a different truth in this posture. Women who wanted friends but didn't go about finding them made the strangest pleas, either with body or with words.

"Have you never looked into someone's eyes?"

No response, again. I reached for her shoulder. She shrugged my hand off. I tugged her by the arm of her jacket. She didn't have an actual arm there, and so she could not pull it away.

"Look at me," I said. "Please."

She gave me a severe and intimidating glance. I couldn't do anything else but smile. Then something in her eyes broke, and she turned away and looked again, and I saw her pupils widen and her brow shake and her eyelids blink. She held her face in her hands and groaned loudly at first and then quietly, the way a kettle settles. When I reached around her shoulder, she looked up from her hands with puffy yellow eyes and her face stained with traces of salt.

"Once upon a time, there was a man who filled me with so much hatred that I grew up knowing nothing else in this world, and I wanted everyone else to see the darkness that was clear to me."

"I can understand that," I said. "The world is very dark, indeed."

"It is," she said. "It absolutely is. But then, there is light, and it lives alongside the shadows in the corners and crevices where no one expects it. Do you know the reason why that is?"

I rubbed my handkerchief over my neck. I sweated the more I thought.

"I assume it is because we all have our light, and we all have our shadow, and neither can be taken away from us until the day we die."

"Perhaps," she said. I took her hand into mine. It was dusty, in need of a serious wash.

"Be honest with yourself," I said. She bit her lip and shook her head.

"I can't," she said. "I've lived so much of my life like a ghost I don't know the first thing about myself."

"That can't be true," I said. Or, if it was, then this was the time for her to start figuring things out.

"It is..." she said. She rubbed her hands like she was starting a flame between them and looked through that long dark path traipsing in the shade. I grabbed her by the elbow.

"Don't look at it," I said, as the light faded in her eyes and the brown of her irises grew. I took her chin in my palm and opened her eyes with my fingers. "I know what it is like to stare at a shadow. You look at it for one second, and you see yourself bigger than you ever were, and you don't know why, but you hate yourself, and you always will. Don't look down in that direction. Your life has been hard, but you have a future. We all do."

She blinked at me with the small wick of someone who had felt their inner candle.

Forgiveness comes for us all,
when we are willing to wait.

She looked to the Great Founder's Plaza,
and strangled the horizon with her one fist.

(The Home Maker)

If I could look back,
I would tell myself one thing.

That a girl
who could take the stance of a desperado
could someday be free.

Don't marry the first man who says he loves you. Take your time. Take at least a year to find out who he is. When he shows you his ugliness once in a while, reflect on it. Don't dismiss it as a momentary lapse, or as something we are all capable of. We are all capable of sin, but we can also control who we marry. He had his temper. He skipped a lot of dates with me because his father told him to study, but if I imagined my life between thirty and sixty, we would be going to literary parties together, drinking wine out of each other's glasses, making quips based on the writings of the novelists we loved or hated. I wasn't going to take my medicine, I wasn't going to take it anymore. What he drove me to was his fault, not mine. How they always tried to lock us away, tear down the wings just as we were learning to fly. I was better. My husband didn't believe me because he didn't believe much of anyone. He had come into the bedroom five minutes earlier to stir the pills into my tea, but I didn't drink it. I told him I was feeling fine, and he didn't have the patience for it, he had a conference on his computer, he was telling us all, and he left the room, making our maid finish his bidding. She had been with us for over thirty years; she knew when I was sick and when I wasn't. Once a week, twice a week, she let me get away with it. Five

(Lyrica)

minutes passed, ten minutes passed, and I didn't take my medicine. Or was it more like half an hour? I stayed in bed because I preferred to have breakfast with my maid. My husband could eat alone.

I wanted more than anything to eat with my husband, but not if it meant eating alone, with him on one side of the dining table and myself on the other. We lived in a three-storey house with over ten rooms. It was made in the image of the palace in the south where I wrote, but that house was full of people, my grandparents, my uncles, my aunties. It was a place where the sun shone not from the sky but from the lake, and the mist the heat brought cleansed the soul. When was the last time I ate surrounded by people? I ate with all of them in my daydreams, but in the rhapsody of my thoughts I knew they were long dead. My father committed suicide, my grandfather committed suicide. My publishers joked that the reason why my biography sold well was because it could be explained: 'Ah, the poor girl, it runs in her family.' In my dreams, my relatives were still very much alive. They extended their hands to each other and waltzed, laughing in reverie, glittering under the stained-glass. They wore humble clothing, but they wore it as if they were in a sybaritic ball. 'Do not trip, my dear girl.' 'Come, my dear daughter, let me show you, this is how you dance, this is how you smile.' I didn't mean to stop waltzing because our maid had knocked. It was because the music I had heard had been turned off.

"Madame, when do you plan to have breakfast?"

"I will have breakfast when my son returns home."

"Madame, I tell you this every day. Your son has not returned home for many years."

"And, I tell you, every day, I will have breakfast when my son returns home."

I was thinking about what I wanted to have for breakfast: puffed rolls, available in the southern part of this country, made especially for the autumn festival, which had passed a week ago, but they weren't available here. The northerners ate flatbreads that I had never found appetising. It had been ages since I had eaten outside. I wanted to drink tea under a parasol, I wanted the wind to puff pollen into my clothes and the sun to bake into my hair. My husband would never agree to it; he thought the moment I went outside I would run and never look back. 'Dearest, the last time you went out, you fainted.' 'Dearest, you are older now, I wouldn't want anything to happen to you.' Excuses. Everything he said was never with a smile. He wasn't a smiler during our courtship, and had never become one. People might change certain aspects of themselves over the course of a life, but never anything that threatens the core. Humans are born with something, and we do everything to do justice to that something, but we dare never change it, and when we did, it was with disastrous results.

It was an interesting line. I took out the notebook from under my bed and wrote it down. I thought the line was wrong; I tore the paper up. 'You're no longer a poet, nothing you write sells anymore.' 'Poets aren't meant to sell; poets are meant to change the world with what they think.' 'Poets are poets when they say something worth saying.' My husband had said all three of these things to me at one point or another, and they all had different meanings. I could divide him into three different people. I did not know him between his birth and the age of twenty-six, but he wasn't a money man when I married him; contrary to how anyone might view him, he adored ballads and the spoken word, and he had gotten into business because his father forced him to. There were only a handful of jobs people could do at that time, and if they chose to do something else, they would have been stuck being poor. Look at him, near age sixty, counting his coins before he goes to bed because he's afraid if he doesn't, our maid will steal them. We sleep in separate rooms, but I know this fact because our maid told me so.

I looked at the pills on my counter, thought about taking them, and remembered I was fine, perfectly fine. I looked outside the window. There was not a cloud in the sky, but the pine trees marched deep into the horizon, in a landscape where there was nothing else for days. The south was a region of much variety, with lakes and forests, hills and mountains, and sand dunes near the coast. One great novelist of the 1890s had called it God's shoulder, because of the diversity of wildlife and plants it protected. No one remembered his name because he was the first one this government ensured to erase. I was there when they took down his statues, burned his books, and punished anyone who promoted him as a traitor to the state. Their tactics worked, or perhaps I had forgotten him because I'd read so many other books since reading his — one every day — and it was hard to remember everyone's names. I kept one of his books hidden under my mattress. Our maid thought it was silly to keep it concealed. 'Dear, no one hunts people for what they read these days.' I cawed at her that no one who wasn't from where we were from could know our suffering, and she tactfully changed the subject.

"Dear, I've come with your breakfast."

"I'm not eating."

She had brought those hard breads with butter and apricot jam, and she was going to do her best to feed me, wearing a bib and putting one over on me because I had the tendency to spit. I was going to be a decent lady. I was going to eat with a fork and knife, crook my little finger, act like a decent northerner. Southerners smiled because they felt their heart beating from morning until night, and they broke the norms of politeness by saying something rude or unpleasant because they felt things that could be easily boxed off. The hard breads had the taste of tar. The jam was not made from fresh-picked fruits, and the butter was harder than my knife. I threw the rest of it against the wall.

"We live in a mansion! You should be able to get the finest jams delivered from the mountains, import any kind of bread in the world."

"The global sanctions make it hard, unfortunately," said our maid and cleaned my mess up.

"I didn't ask you for the news. I want real food. I want my son."

This was another dear secret pressing my heart against its ribcage, that I wanted nothing more than to eat once again with my son, but he was never coming back, and the best I could do was to eat alone. Our maid came from wiping up the mess on the wall to then wiping up my face. As she was cleaning me up, I noticed that she'd missed a bit of jam that had flown onto a portrait of my mother.

"Oh, Mommy dearest, I'm sorry, I'm so sorry! I've made a mess out of everything, like I always do."

'Don't worry, dear. Don't worry, dear.' She never said anything else to me, because she was a quiet woman, beaten out of her opinions through many years together with my father. The poem I wrote about her was the reason why that collection won an international prize. Everyone on the planet called our private number to congratulate me, except my father. This was another thing that made my biography sell well: the idea that he killed himself because he couldn't take what I had said about him. As I replayed these ancient hurts and controversies, I suddenly realised I was hitting the bed with my fist; I was kicking up the blanket and throwing it against the wall.

"I think we should take our medicine," said our maid after she sorted it all.

"No, I'm having a bad day, but I'm not in the mood to run over the garage door. I'm balanced. Think about all the things that happened to me. Wouldn't you be upset?"

"Life is hard on all of us..."

'What are you doing? No daughter of mine is going to pick up a pen!'

"...we simply have to find a way to make peace with ourselves and live on..."

'I tell you, my daughter wants to be a writer. Not a doctor, a writer. Do people read books anymore? She can barely keep her friend's attention. Who's going to listen to a word she says?'

"...I mean, I barely make enough to survive ... but, oh why am I telling you this..."

"I listen very well, thank you very much!"

I threw the tray at her. It wasn't the first time. She threw her hands over her neck and crouched. She was coming to my side, pills cupped in her palm.

"I don't wanna, I don't wanna, I don't wanna!"

She was going to pin me down with the pillow and throw the pills down my throat, but the doorbell was ringing, and my husband wasn't going to get it.

"You think about your health, and you do the right thing," she said, putting the pills on the table right next to my bed. 'Be a responsible girl.' 'Be a good girl.' 'Be a smart girl.' I took all of the pills and crushed the powder out of the capsules with my nails. I wanted to see my husband, but he wasn't going to see me. His eyes never changed after that day I put myself and my son in his car. I remembered the smell of the gasoline, the light feeling in my head, thinking to myself that it would all be over. 'Mommy, I don't feel good.' I told him to keep his seatbelt on; I had thrown the garage opener into a box by the door but I threw away my house keys and heels. 'This is what you get for not loving us!' It must have been around eleven, the wrong time for my husband to get back home. He opened the garage to make way for his second car, didn't look inside of his first one, or notice that his family was inside of it, that the blinkers were on. I cried for that entire time not because my suicide attempt failed, but because he walked around the house for fifteen or twenty minutes before he came out and noticed us.

He thought he could send my son away to boarding school, he thought he could destroy my mind with the pills. He succeeded. My son never came back, and I forgot how to write. I was happy for some time because my son took to writing, in a different form. He wrote in that form well, much better than I, but he was gone; he never called us, he never came back home, and we found out about his success because when he wrote for *Our Nation*, he kept his name. A footnote in his biography implied that when they asked to interview him, he refused and didn't recognise the woman who wrote under the name 'Lyrica' as his mother. They never talk about the men who have made women this way in these biographies. They love to talk about how we failed, how we are damaged and insane, size up our DNA and family history as if we are crustaceans on display, but they forget to mention that my husband talked to his wife and son one or two hours in the week, and that when he did speak, he said the most passive-aggressive things. He never admitted it, but I smelled the cunt of a hooker once on his breath, I knew what they smelled like. He would never admit it; he was an honest and ethical businessman with not a lick of corruption on his fingers. He treated anyone and everyone like a calculation.

Remember, this wasn't the man I married.

I was going back to the window again; I was going to vomit all over the ivies over the sill. I saw that he was smoking from the second storey. I was going to shout at him to get back to his conference, until I saw the flicker of the ashes, the slap to his cheek, the hunger of his lashes, the moments of the man who courted me, and I was twenty-eight all over again, I was in my college dorm writing some things on a scrap of paper, and he was the friend of my roommate who was planning to smoke up with her, but he saw what I was writing, wondered what script it was, asked me to read out loud, and he said he didn't understand a thing but liked how I read. He came the next time with his other friends, and they didn't care much for the sound of my language; they thought it was too liquid in the mouth and hit the eardrums hard, but I translated it. He told me few can master one language, let alone several. This was something written about me in the newspapers, in the book reviews, and my award citation, but the first one who said it was the first shell of my husband, molted over the years for him so he become successful at what his father loved.

"I hate you, I hate you, I hate you!" I shouted after opening the window. He extinguished his cigarette on the windowsill and looked up at me.

"Did you not take your medicine? I told you to take it."

"Did you not listen to me? I said I hate you!"

"You say this to me every day. You would remember if you took your pills."

What I wanted to say was, 'I love you, I love you, I love you!' but for that his actions would have to change.

"You've been putting me on these pills since the day I tried to kill myself, but what you never did was listen to me. Don't you feel sorry for what you did?"

He closed the window.

"It must not be easy, being married to me. You thought I was brilliant, you thought I was charming, until you realised I was a human being. You were this close to divorcing me, but you never went through with it. You threw the papers in my face, you sent our son away to boarding school. You think I did what I did for attention? I bet it's the reason why you stayed married to me!"

My husband was coming from the other side of the door, pushing me against the wall, back into my bed.

"We have this conversation once a week, and I am not in the mood to have it now. You take your pills and go to sleep."

He was going to do it like he had done a few days ago, hit me with the pillow, throw me onto the bed, push those pills into my mouth, cover my lips with his hand.

"I'm not a toy, I'm not a toy, I'm not a toy!"

Our maid was barging in, doing something she would never do otherwise, pulling my husband off me, pushing him towards the door.

"Do you want some time alone with him? Please, kiss him by the door; I can hear the sounds you two make by the stairwell."

"This isn't the time for this!" our maid shouted. "Make yourself presentable, act like normal people. Your son has finally come home!"

My husband's eyebrows were collapsing into a puddle on the floor.

"What?" he said, summoning himself out. This was step two of their plans, to tell me my son was home, and the shock of it being a lie would force me to have a heart attack, and I would die, and my husband would get something out of the insurance, the maid could sleep in my bed. We went down all three flights of stairs in line and into the foyer, a red room decorated on all sides by marble statues and fake flowers. I was ready to tell them I knew what they were planning, and I wasn't going to let them, I was going to divert myself into the garage, take his car, leave for good.

A man somewhere in his thirties was sitting on the couch. His hair was cut in the shape of a schoolboy's. 'Why are you making me take a lunchbox to school? No one takes them anymore.' The shades of it were greyer than my husband's. 'You're going to go bald if all you do is work all day.' His socks were not matching; one was black and the other was violet. 'Stop touching me! I like wearing my socks like this, it makes me look like I can attack!' His brown skin was one shade darker than mine. 'I'm not a sandman, I'm not a sandman, I'm a human being!'

This was not the day he was supposed to come back. He was supposed to come back someday after boarding school instead of taking a scholarship to the capital that left him there. He was supposed to take a job writing for the newspaper of this city, not the capital, and work in something less dangerous and investigative. He was supposed to die with me on that day. I was supposed to die with him, but I stayed here and rotted inside of myself, while he came back to this house more than reborn.

He was wearing the plaid shirt my father wore, carrying a basket of puffed rolls.

"My boy, my boy, my boy," my husband shrank into his son's arms, held him by the neck, rested his son into his shoulder. He had nothing else to say, his eyes were watering and wandering.

"I'm home, Mom," he said.

"I see that," I said. I did not cry; I had done that too much and our maid was doing it for me. A bowling ball could have been rolled into my chest, a thousand ceilings could crumble over my skull, and I was going to stand, wait for this boy to tell me what he wanted out of me, and give it to him, exactly. I wasn't going to hug him yet, I wasn't going to say sorry, I hadn't earned that right that afternoon, I wasn't going to earn it within a day or a week. "What have you been doing all these years?"

"Writing, working. I was in your hometown for some months."

"I saw the articles. They were very nice."

I had to rub my eyes. It was like having two red flowers pressed against my eyelids, the colours glimmering what I didn't want to see.

"Thank you. I think I will go back next spring. I hope we can go together. Your cousin sent this basket for you. They were handmade by her daughter. She never forgot how much you loved them."

"I forgot I had a cousin who was alive at all."

"Mother, are you okay?"

I was collapsing, I was fainting, I was getting hit by the emotions in each and every part of my nerves. It was just like when we were in that car and there was more gas inside of him than in me. My son picked me up. He had learned to speak a lot more, he had learned to present himself with heart. He carried me up by the legs; he was a strong boy, he was a man. Our maid was telling him to take me into my bedroom, she was telling me I needed my medicine, I needed to rest. It would be okay to sleep off. No matter how much I closed my eyes, all I remembered was his thirteen-year-old body in the back of the car, seconds away from dead, before my husband opened the garage, coincidentally. I deserved the last thirty years to be a punishment, to be whipped by the devils, have my mind surrendered to their pickings, knowing that this was their ultimate retribution, to have me imagine a moment with my son in a daydream, right before my life was taken.

(Lyrica)

I awoke shortly after,
under the same yellow sheets.

No matter how much I closed my eyes,
all I did was remember.
Her long braid crossed her neck
towards her chest,
her hand covered the flare-up of acne
around her breasts.

My son was by my side,
holding my hand,
promising with his grip
he wasn't giving up on me easily.

My mother smelled like she came from picking beets,
and the rooster had come to snuggle between us.
I did not want to be anywhere else but in this cot,
enveloped in my mother's arms.

I held on,
willing to give up my bones
if it meant we could rewind to
seventeen years ago,
start over again.

"Sorry, sorry, sorry," I was saying to my mother,
over and over again, the way I had done at daybreak when
my father came back home at four in the morning with the
police to tell me that the girl they thought was my best
friend, the milkmaid, was found hung over the second
floor of her family's cow estate, and she didn't understand
what for.

"Dear, what are you apologising for? Your friend has
died, it is horrible, we are all sad as well, but it's not your
fault."

She was picking at the follicles on my scalp and
removing stray hairs. I remembered how my father had told
us how they had found a lot of unpaid bills, a stained cot on
the floor, a high definition television with a cracked screen,
and a lot of empty alcohol bottles. My father said the police
were questioning him like he was a suspect, but he knew
they really just wanted their bribe. After he paid them off,
they dismissed him, and went on their way to call some
other rich member of the community. He didn't stop

complaining about the police, and my mother reminded him to be sensitive. I wanted to ask if they found her diary, but I never had it in me to ask. I asked if I could lie down, and my mother affirmed, and she went to lie with me. I only got up once, and that was to vomit in the privacy of our toilet, and to stare at myself in the mirror. I might have been away for longer than an hour, because my mother pried the door open and forced me to return to rest with her in the cot. I couldn't fall asleep. I wouldn't fall asleep. The dawn became the morning, and the morning became noon, and I ate when my mother asked me to, but I wasn't feeling hungry at all. Some of my friends came over.

"Hey, it's okay if you don't want to say anything, and it sucks what happened. We really understand. But, can we take the box? We feel like trying on some wigs."

I just sighed and let them take it. The noon became the afternoon. I said I wanted to take a walk a few hours later. My mother hugged me hard.

"No, you cannot go. I'm afraid of who's out there, hurting little girls."

"No one killed her. She killed herself."

My mother slapped me.

"Don't you dare speak of such sinful things. You must be hallucinating; you haven't slept at all."

I sat alone on my cot, pretending to watch TV. I wondered why she didn't ask me why I thought it was a suicide.

The milkmaid had been a fine girl until she met me. She had her worries like everyone else, and I didn't think much about them because I was a kid too, but she grew up, busty and pretty, and I grew to hate a person who saw me as a person who she could be herself with. Because I hated her, I betrayed her. I was the reason she did what she did. I was the reason why she was crushed, and why everyone who loved her had to be crushed as well. Why didn't I say anything to the police? I was a worm cut in half. I squirmed a lot on the cot and kept my eyes closed because I had so much to say but didn't know how to express any of it.

I was going for the door. I saw my father and mother outside, inspecting a new table he had carved on the patio of our house. My mother must have been staring at it, but she turned around to look at me.

"Hey! I told you not to leave! Come back, come back here, now!"

I respected her more than she knew. She had gotten old in recent years, and she could forget where she put her medication or even the names of the cousins she had raised. But she could never forget to be sweet, or how to spoil me. I used to think that she forgot my age for how much she treated me like a child, and then this all happened, and she came to my cot and kissed my fingers and held them to her face and asked me to start crying, and it was like I was always her child, and I would be that child for eternity.

I was leaving, and they didn't chase me. They had every reason to stop me. I had bumped into the wooden tables and it had been infested with termites, and the table toppled over with my touch. They didn't say a single word. I didn't see the termites, but I imagined them crawling at me and gnawing at my bones the way they eat through wood. I passed all of the other shacks to get to the creek, and I didn't hear people. I just heard the busy mandibles of the termites.

I must have looked horrible. My hair needed to be brushed. My tear ducts were caked in mucus like someone who had just gotten up. I was holding a doll in my hands, and I was too tall for the clothes I was wearing, this sun-patterned skirt and white T-shirt that we wore together at a younger age, like what she wore that day when she killed herself.

"Hello, cousin! How are y— oh, dear, I'm sorry. You're not my cousin at all."

Were those the thoughts of these termites in my mind, or was I hearing the shepherd's son speak to me through crooked teeth as I passed him and his flock?

People never did recognise me. I wasn't that pretty, and I saw a lot of other faces that looked like mine. I was tall, rare for women here, and my father was considered one of the best carpenters in the area, with one of the richest-looking houses. It wasn't enough. The boys looked right through me, and the girls barely remembered me. It didn't matter how often I invited them to my house or how often I lent them the magazines of my older sister in the city and dressed them up in her makeup and wigs. To prove my point, I knocked on the window of the mud shack between the field and the creek. One of the girls who had come to the gathering last week was sitting with her brother watching the morning cartoons, and she was eating some of the porridge her mother was cooking on a pot over a fire outside. She opened her window to talk to me.

"Oh, hey! How are you?"

"I'm good, thanks."

"Great."

This was our conversation, and it was because I knocked that she looked up, and when she looked up, she looked down first and went back to her cartoons until she noticed it was me.

I was nothing to them. I had gotten rid of my only enemy who was my only friend, and somehow, everything was the same.

The stares were the worst around the creek. Between the creek and this set of mud huts was a trail that led to the main road. Women from all parts of the area used this road to get to the creek. They carried dirty pots and pans, tubs of laundry, or a child in one hand and various cleaning products in the other. The two or three who passed by were too busy to pay me any attention. I did overhear a little bit of their conversation.

"I heard that her father molested her, and tried to drink the milk from her nipples and called her his cow."

"I heard her father brought prostitutes to the house to act like her mother. It is no surprise they had no money to pay the bills, then. Can you imagine it, a prostitute, a mother? Bah!"

"Ah, yes, yes, what a shame, the poor girl. No wonder she went on a path where there was no turning back. Only praying can save her now."

"And, this question about her having a disease?"

Why couldn't I go up to them and tell them it was all lies? I used to think women told lies about other women when they were sitting around a fire and washing pots or cooking porridge and had nothing else to do for the rest of the day. Then, I lied about my best friend, the kind of lies men told each other if one man had a shop that was doing well. Some of these men were on their way to the main road. They glanced at me and stared back onto their path. It was like their eyes looked mad because they wanted to return to their thoughts but they had to think of the strange sight of a young girl in an undersized T-shirt carrying a doll for babies. I would have given anything for them to stare at me because they thought I was worth looking at.

The place where I burned the doll was nothing like the part of the creek where we used to do it. The creek used to be very green, but a lot of trees were cut down, and the part of the creek nearest our shacks was open to the plains. This part of the land ascended and split, and the more it was covered in trees, the more I would see the girls who were walking behind the rocks to bathe. I chose a spot behind one of the bigger rocks. It was big enough for people behind it to kiss their girlfriends or pee. I sat in the grass and took one of the matches hidden under my skirt. I looked at this doll made of straw and clothed with nylon. I remembered how my mother painted it with wide green eyes and a beaming red smile while I was learning arithmetic. People were staring towards that rock because a little of my forehead peeked out from over it, and I was breathing loudly.

I thought of her for the longest time as a boy, and I talked to her once walking back from school on the main road because I was going through a collection phase where I wanted every girl to think highly of me. I lied the entire time. I told her I loved the length of her hair, when I saw every older man staring at it and wanted to chop it off. I told her I wished my mother would buy me an orange and yellow dress like hers, when really I just wanted to take every fake diamond on the corner of each colour and chip it. I made wishes to have the grace of her strides when she walked, when she walked like more of a man than some of the boys. I assured her I wanted to do nothing but hang out with her when I had time, and she took it seriously. She asked me if I had watched anything burn. I chuckled and thought about how strange this girl was when she led me into the forest and lit that doll on fire while she held it in her hand. The burning doll smelled like lipstick, and the flames shooting out of it were brighter than any other fire, and I screamed and cackled and held her hand as it sputtered and crackled and combusted.

I held that doll in my hand and lit the match against it. The truth was this. Her mother was one of the workers hired by her father, and she died from the same disease that killed him later. She couldn't take it one day and told me this. She also told me she was afraid of the hives on her arms and the bills she had to pay. She asked if she could sleep over at my house someday, the way the young girls did. I heard everything she said, and I did say yes, but before saying all this, she had bragged about how many marriage proposals she received in a day, and I was paying more attention to how well her breasts fit inside her dress.

I stood a bit away from the rock and held the fire against the doll's feet.

Fire is a ravenous creature. It consumes itself like temptation at the first thing it touches. It sparks and crackles and sputters, and clouds the carcass of what it has eaten with smoke. I felt the taste of burnt flesh at the tip of my tongue, sucked on my own spit and wandered my tongue around my cheeks. The taste remained. As for my own skin, it might as well have been my body that burned. The nature of heat was like that. The closer it came, the more you felt like you were getting scorched by the sun, and your muscles shook, and your eyeballs dried, and you wanted to get as far away as you could. It was an instinct, not something you could control.

I wasn't moving. I was going to get what I deserved.

(The Carpenter's Daughter)

I told myself this.

Over the carcass of my husband,
the skeletons of my parents underneath,
the lumps of branches and twigs and moss,
this part of our soul we called a home.

I was never going to spread another rumour in my life.
I was never going to speak out against another person
no matter how much I hated her or wanted to ruin her life.

We summoned the sticks together to make fire,
we did so with our hands on the turtle flesh,
to provide food for our children,
not to provide the flame to bury them in.

I was no longer going to push people away.
I was going to show my family I appreciated them
in different ways
at least once a week.

What did my mother say once?
If you fall to emotion this often,
you will never be of any use.
If you do not eat what you are given,
you can eat nothing at all.

I was going to smile once in a while.

I thought of all the moons
I slept under her bones,
and now her bones were burning with the hut.

I was going to learn to love my face,
and love my height,
and love my nose,
and love my every other not-so-great feature.

It was getting to be too much.
I stammered to myself
as my feet sank deeper into the earth,
looked at who was left of my family,
my daughter, her three daughters, her two sons,
showed the weakness of my spirit to them all.

I was going to learn to love myself,
And others.

And, then, I let the fire burn.
Our tent could no longer be called proud. What was left of
the grass and wood was a singed stain of black, crumpled
and piled onto the silt. I wanted to claw underneath, dig up
my family's bones, but the fire still burnt, and by the time it
rained, I would be gone, my children would be gone, their
children would be gone. The mud would consume these
flakes as fire did our home; the river would drink from our
remains and birth bubbles of life; roots of the underwater

(The Elder)

trees would find a way to grow. The sadder fact was I had no history to tell, and I had lived on this land longer than some of the trees.

And, then, "Come, mother," said my youngest daughter.

And, then, "Come, grandmother," repeated one of my granddaughters. They both tugged at an arm. Most of my family was taken by the skin-eating disease. One of my grandsons realised that I would come soon after, for I was sleeping longer, and my head felt hot, the way my son's body did before it erupted into bumps. I told him they could burn me with the tent, I was an old woman, I was in no position to escape, but as the ablest of my sons came from his tent to cut down trees with their knives and as another carved canoes for his own sons and daughters, he refused to leave me behind. He did not realise the more I aged, the more I was convinced I did not need to be near others to know they were around. It was as if my spirit had grown tethered to the earth itself and felt the tap of any foot with the pulse of my blood. The sweet housewives who gossiped with me under the moon, who took their time to help me cook the fish, as my pruned fingers were quick to succumb to burn, they were gone, as was my husband, as were his other wives, as was one of my daughters, as were two of my sons, all buried beneath that tent as it burnt. My children, my children! If there was one skull I needed to press against my own in times of need, it belonged to the one woman who knew what to say in dire times, my grandmother. They let her bones lie buried underneath that fire, with everyone else, and no matter how much I begged, they let them burn.

And, then, I said, as they were dragging me through the finger trees, as the monkeys were hopping between the branches in the direction of the river as well, "Let go of me."

My daughter said, "Never. We have to go." I said, "You should have let me take them with us." My grandchild said, "We do not have time for this. The chief and his warriors are hunting deserters. We will all be dead if we stay here. We must go." I pulled with all my strength towards our home, but they could hold me down as if I were the leaf of a branch. No, it was worse than being the leaf of a branch. I was a fallen, dried leaf being dragged towards the river by a light breeze. I saw the strange footprints my feet made in the mud as if they belonged to some beast of a story. I was not going to act like a child being forced to bathe. I turned to face the jungle and took steps of my own. It was no surprise that I tripped shortly after.

And, then, my youngest son said, "You carried me when I broke my leg. It is my turn to carry you." He lifted me with greater force than I ever had. I wanted to cry. I did not remember this story in question, but my youngest son, who became too occupied after his marriages, had abandoned his mother to his wives and family, and was one of the weakest boys I had seen. He did not cry during his circumcision ceremony, but he spent many moons after it begging for the purple berries to be fed from my hand to his mouth. He trained to be a hunter but was chased by the monkeys and turtles more than he chased after them. He had in the end no set purpose for this tribe, and lived in his tent and did as he pleased, which gave reason for me to believe that he should have spent more time with his mother. I was not in a position to complain; I had already lost many kin. I was also not in a position to discipline. We were in a situation on the precipice of life and death, for not one individual but for the remaining members of our bloodline, yet the two or three of his wives walking behind me were cackling petty remarks about each other.

And, then, we crossed the path of silt. I didn't remember the path to the river being this quick. In my young days, we didn't have anything cleared between the river and the tents. The line of finger trees was long enough; we would have to cross many to see a cliff, and this cliff peered into the water, a gushing dark blue, and we stepped through the silt steps to wade in the water and fish. The finger trees were cleared because we needed more huts. The chief of that time had grown ambitious, taking the land of this tribe or that one, forcing the slaves to live here and not in their lands. The spirits of their ancestors cursed us for what we did to their progeny; our people were not made to live with them, and having so many people living together was too much of a burden on the land. I asked my son, "Do you believe our tribe is suffering as a consequence of all the bad decisions our leaders have made?" My son was ducking in between the vines, taking care to make sure my head did not hit against any of the trees. He said, "This is a deep question, Mother. I have never thought about it before. I don't see why I should begin to think about it when we will never see this land again." I asked him later, "Won't you miss the berries we grew outside of our tent? What about the distinct taste of the turtle found on this side of the river and nowhere else?" My son paused. His son was in front of us angling his spear for enemies. He said, "We don't have the time to stand."

And, then, we reached the bank of the river. Six out of the twenty families were on the silt. The men were taking the canoes they had built in the jungle and were waddling them onto the water. Some wives were strong enough to help, as the frail and elderly comforted their children or grandchildren. I was the eldest of our tribe. Time was not to be wasted, yet a member from each family came to my son's feet, kneeled to the ground, blew the sand towards me. I was tearing up. These were the values of our tribe, and my sons were right: they needed to see many more generations. My eldest son, who was also the swiftest, was here much earlier. He pulled his feet from under the trunk of his canoe, bent himself to his family, and kissed both of my hands. His wife could not touch her husband, but she saw how I was looking, and she had a tear in her eye as well. Everyone took turns kissing me on the cheek — my sons, my daughters, my granddaughters, my grandsons, their cousins, their uncles, their aunts, their nephews, their nieces. Our tears were not to be wasted. The smoke from the fires billowed above the canopy of trees.

And, then, someone ran from the other side of the clearing and said, "Hurry, the warriors are coming." In the near distance we heard the echoes of arrows splattering into silt. My son was running with me in his arms. I was not surprised when he tripped. My premonitions were getting stronger. The older I got, the more connected I was to invisible tendrils in the air, and it was in those moments of connection that the spirits told me what was to come. I was not going to live much longer. I told my son, "Don't worry about me. I already told you to leave me to burn with our ancestors." My daughter cried, "You are our mother. You are one of the few we have left. We thank the spirits you are too old to move your legs, for we will never leave you, and never let you be left." I told them, "The spirits are talking to me more and more. This is a sign I will no longer be in this world." I did not tell them that the spirits told me other things. They had long warned me our tribe was too big and too proud. They had also warned me of the thatched man's disease and the coming wars. What they told me the moon was a revelation: many would die, but one out of seven would live on, taking the skin in the form a man yet unknown to us.

And, then, the warriors arrived. They shot some of the men in the neck. Their heads sunk into the bodies of their canoes and the blood dripped ochre into the pulse of the river. As for the men who were coming up to flail their arms at the warriors, they were immediately flayed by the knife. The men nearer to the silt were throwing rocks. Some who had been taught bow and arrow were shooting back. The warriors were too busy to bother with an old woman and her family. My son was carrying me; my granddaughter was leading me by the hand to one of the canoes. I kicked my feet in protest. I said, "You can't carry me. You won't be fast enough. Leave me to die here. This is the land of my fathers, my grandfathers, their fathers, and their fathers as well. My bones were meant to be buried alongside theirs. Do not deny me my wish."

Arrows rained from the bows of the second wave of the warriors, and my son who was carrying me was shot in the back. We were between the water and the silt; he fell against the canoe and tossed my back against its trunk. I groaned and I shuddered from the pain, until I remembered that my son was dying. I screamed to the spirits to give him life. After having seen so many of my kin die in front of my eyes, I did not want one more; I did not want it to be this son. He had lost consciousness; perhaps by the time I had finished reeling, he had drowned. His wife pulled me up and forced me into the canoe. Her children were pushing the canoe into the deeper water, as fog ruffled in the wind and covered the riverside in mist.

Out of the fog came the eyes of flame from the skull of the grand chief. Next came his dented spear, in the hand of the current chief. The weapon had been newly christened with blood akin to the colour of the feathers in his crown. He was not with his slaves or his wife or his sons. He was alone. He commanded, "You are not to take a single step." Yet, every single man or woman who was conscious was pushing their canoes out of the silt. What a failure this chief had come to be. I had known his father, and little of his cunning or charisma had been passed on. This chief had no talent for governance, but wanted to call this land his alone. He was a man who would sacrifice the lives of his tribe for the sake of his ego; he had already torn the hearts from babies predicted to be shamans and drank their blood, all to guarantee his rule. I shouted from my canoe, "We are the ones born from your father, and your father's father, and the fathers of those who came before them. They are your brothers, your very kin, and if you slay us, it does not matter what spirit you profess to placate. You are no chief to this tribe!"

The chief threw his spear into the back of my daughter, who had been doing everything to push me to safety. Her head collapsed onto the canoe and stared at me as I screamed. I swore for a moment that my heart had stopped. To see directly into the eyes of your child in the very moment she experiences her death is a wound to both spirit and flesh. What was worse was knowing I had no time to react. I had made an enemy of the chief; in a moment of pure brashness I had endangered the lives of all of my remaining kin. The chief was stampeding towards my canoe, and my grandchildren, strong as they were for their age, were not strong enough to dislodge a carved tree trunk from the sands. The spirits did not need to speak to me for me to become aware of what was to come next. He would stab my son, the one who was already facing him with a knife guarding my rear, then kill or capture whichever progeny of mine defended me next. After this he would drag me back to the corner by his warriors and force me to watch him rape, dismember, and kill my family members. I had seen enough death. I was ready to take the knife from my son's clenched fist and cut my own throat.

Just then, an arrow cut through a bend of the mist like light. It struck the chief in the shoulder, and before he could react, another arrow pierced him in the rib cage. The chief crawled towards the water's edge and his crown fell into the river. He dragged himself with the help of his spear and reached around to pull the arrows out of his shoulder and back, but as he did, three more arrows struck him. He could no longer crawl. He turned onto his back and flung sand over his wounds as he tried to speak through bubbles of blood. The short one who shot him walked out of the fog and collapsed to the chief's side. It was not a warrior; it was not the Silencer.

"You have done your best, but I have spent the last moon with the spirits. As they killed the boy who cried for no reason, they told me everything you had done, and everything wrong about it. They told the boy who was reborn the true path for our people. I will no longer allow you to lead us to ruin."

The chief raised his arms and tried to strangle him. The boy kissed his father on the left cheek and on the right, and he kissed him on the forehead, and he picked up the spear his father tried to hold, and he stabbed him in the throat. The blood spurted out of his body and onto the legs and chest and groin of his son. The mist of the river was thick; we could feel its drizzle on our skin. The son of this chief pulled out the spear and grabbed the corona from the waves. He tucked his grandfather's skull under his arm. With his feet sinking prints on the silt, he tapped his grandfather's spear twice against the sand and stared into the eyes of each and every one of us.

"My people. Now speaks the man destined to make the great cats bow to feet, now speaks the man who will lock eyes with the sun. I have found our new land. Take your canoes and follow me. A new time for our tribe has come."

Not a single man found it in himself to raise a weapon, nor did a single wife open her mouth. The eyes of the eternal shone not from the skull but from the eyes of our chief's first son. We believed that the spirits had bestowed him with our future. He had the eyes of life and death and life once more.

Acknowledgements

To anyone who knows me, *we of the forsaken world...* has been my labour of love since 2011. I was on a bus between Dubrovnik and Zagreb when a svelte woman (tall, brunette, with a lingering stare) sat down next to me on one of the stops. We began to talk about a host of things I can't remember now. The one thing that she told me which did remain in my head was the following: *Croatia is one of the poorest countries in the world.* Something about that sentence inspired my imagination. We reached the bus station, but I was not able to leave. I had to sit on one of the metal benches for a few hours. I was starting to imagine five different countries, completely imagined in my head, and I could not stop myself from writing about them. One was a war-torn Eastern European country. The other could have been any dirty megalopolis in a third-world country. There was a town that wasn't so different looking from my grandmother's place, the southern Indian city of Mysore. There was a tribe in the middle of nowhere, and a town destroyed by an industrial spill. I also imagined hundreds of voices. I wanted to tell them all, in the space of one book.

In 2011, that book was composed of five regions and featured one-hundred-and-fifty voices. Despite the amount of territory covered, the first draft was only three hundred pages. Most of my characters were thinly veiled rants, in the form of vignettes. The language was powerful and poetic, but the book had little sense of story. Over the next few years, my novel was significantly trimmed down. I made it four regions instead of five. My hundred-and-fifty voices became a hundred, then eighty-something, then fifty, then thirty-two, then sixteen. I kept working to ensure that only the most nuanced and individualised voices "survived." I also tried to make sure each vignette added substance to the four centralising characters of the book: the one-armed woman, the journalist, the chief's son, and the milkmaid. I found that most of my characters were repetitive. I also found that rather than making one character give a small piece of the greater story, I could have a section reveal greater chunks of life. Once my box of voices became a chain of sixteen, it no longer felt like an epic novel, but something between a novel and a collection of short stories. Though I originally wanted *we of the forsaken world...* to be more sprawling and more epic than it finally became, I am satisfied at the place it ended up at. I consider the space between the story and the novel to be an especially ripe one for telling the interconnected tales of those at the peripheries of our globalising world, and I wanted to take advantage of this space, that structure, to web through the stories of the nameless in our borderless planet, and show how people with unconnected lives can live in sync sometimes with people who don't even share the same place of origin.

Many people helped me bring this book into its current form. Most of these were developmental editors, who took a stake in making sure my worlds were more profound rather than unnecessarily large. Some of them I hired, while others were agents or editors who were doing me a favour. Others were good friends who happened to love to read. In no particular order, I thank J.T. Kent, Xiao Yu, Wendy Rohm, Roz Foster, Tom Mayer, Christopher Lueker, Robyn Russell, Jason Buchholz, Nathan Rostron, and Mark Miller for being of great help during this time of struggle. I also want to thank some people who read the manuscript and gave advice that later proved useful. In this space, I would also like to thank those who tried their best to get me opportunities in the literary world, even if they never actualised. These are Ranjan Venkatesh, Mikra Krasniqi, Nina Gabrielan, Banu Vaughn, Anukul Tripathi, Jagdish Sheth, Vikas Swarup, and Yuyutsu Sharma. I must thank the places of Mysore, São Paulo, Manu Jungle, Malindi, Lake Van, and Jogjakarta. Inhabiting these places was very useful in the conceptualisation of these four worlds, and I would like to believe a lot of scenes in the book bear a close relationship to things that could actually happen within these cultures. My humble thanks to Bobo Bose-Kolanu, Ishita Patel Kent ("who judged me so hard I had to write this so she'd stop"), Janaki Challa, and my various cousins, aunties, and uncles, who have been there for me the longest, and have had to hear me whine about this book the most. I give a special thanks to my parents, who really have worked hard to understand their writer son, to love me, and to make sure I would be successful on my chosen path. Finally, I have to thank Lee Parpart and Greg Ioannou for giving this book a home at Iguana Books.